OF REUNIONS

Kenneth A. Strickland

KAS Publishing

&

Mythical Legends Publishing

A KAS Publishing and Mythical Legends Publishing Trade Paperback Edition

Copyright © 2015 by Kenneth A. Strickland
Published by **KAS** and
Mythical Legends Publishers, 2016
Publisher@mythicallegends.com
http://mythicallegends.com

ISBN-10: 1-943958-52-1
ISBN-13: 978-1-943958-52-8

Printed in the United States of America
9 8 7 6 5 4 3 2 1

DEDICATION

This book is dedicated to all the great dreamers
Who taught me how to dream . . .
That includes my dad (who said it was okay to be who I was),
every book I've ever read, every movie I've ever seen,
. . . And every dream that I ever had the chance to remember
. . .

ACKNOWLEDGEMENTS

To all those who are on this journey with me . . .

Of Reunions

CHAPTER ONE

LOSS AND DISCOVERY

Michael John Stone sat in the darkened apartment. It wasn't much, just a small two-bedroom place that allowed father and son to have their own rooms for once in their lives. It had been nice.

"Is anybody alive in here besides me?" Michael cried out in the empty room. "I'd like someone to talk to that's older than ten years old!" He picked up the phone and listened for the dial tone. It was dead.

Oh yeah.

The phone company turned it off, saying they didn't knowingly deal with fraud artists. The bank froze his accounts, the ones he'd spent two years building up, saying the same thing.

What had he done? If he had done something, who did he do it to?

His dream job working at Hamilton Film Effect Studios as a miniature builder and computer operator was lost. His calling card film was declared plagiarized.

"Mike, I'm sorry." Jake Hamilton told him after he pulled him into his office, "but this guy says you stole his film." Jake pointed at a pock faced, scraggly looking eighteen-year-old kid. Michael thought if this guy, whose name he didn't know, found his ass it was because someone showed him where it was.

"Jake, I can show you everything! As a matter of fact, I did!" Michael shouted.

Shaking his head sadly Jake closed the door. "Mike I know you showed me. Trouble is he showed me the same thing. The exact same thing. Look I can't afford to get into a shit fight. Things are tight right now. If I get into the middle of this it could shut me down."

Michael staggered back. "Jake," he started to plead.

"Mike, I'm sorry." Jake said. "Look, I have your two week severance. Look, you can wait a couple of weeks let it blow by until you can prove he's lying, or you can reapply with me."

"Forget it! If I reapply and you hire me, he can drag you through the mud." Michael said.

"I know. I'm just saying, wait a week or two. Once this guy washes out I can rehire you." Jake told him.

"Yeah, and what will the other guys say? The black guy couldn't do it without cheating someone else." Michael fumed. "Or else they will say I stole from him and intimidated him so bad he was scared to come forward until now. Either way, I'm screwed."

"I can write you a letter of recommendation." Jake began.

"Don't bother. This will get out before I can." Michael said. He stalked to the door and left the office. He deliberately bumped into the kid and knocked him down.

"Damn it all." Jake said as he watched. Mike showed talent. He could see Michael directing some day. Now it was all gone.

Michael went to his desk, packed his tools, grabbed his Raiders coat. It had been cold out. Now as far as he was concerned it was freezing. He shook Jake's hand and a few of the others who let him know they believed it was all bullshit. He left Hamilton Studios for good after almost a year.

Michael went to the bank to check on his accounts. He should not have been surprised to find out his accounts were frozen. The bank official was cold and efficient and told him the IRS was investigating him. His recently earned credit cards were taken from him and he was shown the door.

Michael walked out wondering what he was going to live on. All he had now was the severance check and what little he had in his pockets.

Michael made his way back to his apartment wondering what was going on. To his knowledge he had no ongoing arguments with anyone. There were no recent wrongs done.

"I feel like London after the blitz." Michael sank lower in his chair. The sun was setting when he heard the lock to the front door.

Ralton.

Ralton John Stone was all of ten years old, almost eleven. Coming into the apartment, he hit the light switch and nothing. Looking around, he spotted his father in his favorite chair, frowning. "Dad, what's going on? Didn't you pay the light bill?"

The frown intensified. "Kid, it's been a bad day." He spotted the package in his son's arm. "Whatchu got?"

"I don't know if you still want it. It's your birthday present." Ralton answered. "Happy birthday, I think."

Michael smiled at his son and ran his fingers through his son's hair. It was Jessie's hair.

Both Michael and Jessie were fifteen. He was a virgin. She was well practiced.

Jessie was also curious about him; Michael was black all right, but his cheekbones were sharp and well defined and his eyes were a deep blue-green. Those eyes brought him much grief and teasing. Many of his classmates thought he wore contact lenses. He did have a black man's full sensual lips and his nose was typical. Standing five foot eleven in his stocking feet, well-muscled from years of hard work, he was deeply ambitious. He wanted college and a film career. His eyes and grasp were set far ahead of most of his classmates. He didn't succumb to Jessie's obvious charms.

She was a charmer, indeed. Café-au-lait skin, smooth and silky with laughing brown eyes over a perfect nose and full sensitive lips. Jessie was good looking and she knew it. She didn't even have to flaunt it. She discovered sex at an early age and truly enjoyed it. She didn't have sex with every boy she met, just the ones she liked. Jessie LaNisha Williams liked a lot of boys.

Michael was surprised when Jessie showed an interest in him. Every alarm in his mind told him this could be trouble. He went for the trouble.

In the back of Michael's used Chevy van (he'd just gotten his license three months earlier. After working on the van for a year to get it running, Michael took Jessie on a date. Mike explored Jessie to the best of his meager ability and the fullest of pleasure. They did it three times slowly as Michael followed every instinct telling him to take his time. Jessie helped by showing him how to make all the right moves. They were lucky it was a Friday night. Michael drove her home even though she made him drop her off a block away. He followed at a discrete distance to make sure she got home safely. She waved to the back of the disappearing van before going inside. For a moment she leaned against the front door and thought, he was way better than she thought he would be. For his part, Michael thought he got very lucky. He was glad he wasn't her boyfriend. He hated to think she would be like that with every guy she went out with.

Four weeks later, she shocked him with the news she was pregnant and he was the father.

Michael knew the baby was his. He couldn't say how he

knew, he simply knew.

Jessie's father was ready to kill him.

Michael made her an offer. Deliver a live birth and he would give her the money in his college account. He showed them how much he had. It would go into a nine month CD and she would get it only if she delivered. If she aborted she would get nothing.

Bill Williams protested loudly saying his daughter didn't need to have a baby for money. Jessie figured, why not if Michael was willing to pay for it.

Michael had the papers drawn up. Jessie signed, as did he. Michael didn't say why he wanted this baby. He was afraid that he would never have a child and this was a chance to have his family. He knew it was crazy but he didn't see any other way.

Nine months later Michael watched as his son Ralton John Stone came into the world. He held the baby in his arm and cried. Jessie was surprised the baby meant that much to him. Michael turned the money over in a certified check. Jessie signed custody over to the new father. Michael thanked her and took the baby home to the room behind the garage at his aunt's house.

His mind returning to the present, Michael gave a wan smile to his son and sighed deep and heavy. "Son o' mine, I've got bad news. First, I've lost my job. Second, we've got to move in two weeks. I don't know how we're going to do it since the bank froze my money. Lord above us all, I don't know what I'm going to do. I had enough of Bertha in the two years we lived with her." He opened his birthday gift. It was a book, "LAW AND CHAOS" by Wendy Pini. "Thanks."

"I could afford it at the time." Ralton turned thoughtful. "It sounds like that bad movie I saw on television last night."

"Six o'clock." Michael said looking at his watch. "If I'm going to starve, I'd do better on a full stomach. What say we get a pizza?"

"I'll eat to that." Ralt said.

"I thought you would." Michael got on his coat and checked for his keys. He also slipped on his studded leather gloves just in case.

When they were gone, two men stepped out of the closet. It wasn't a closet, it was a dimensional tesseract generated by a device that gave you more room in the same space. It was handy for making sure you had the room you needed. If Michael and Ralton could see inside of it, they would see many people working in there speaking a strange language. The two men who stepped out of the space surveyed the room. They younger of the two went to the window and cracked open the shade. He saw the father and son make their way down the street. "They are gone my lord." He said as he turned to face his companion. "They will take about an hour if they go to the pizza restaurant three blocks down. If he holds true, he will indulge in an ice cream cone afterwards."

"That is true. It's plenty of time to rearrange this room and remove the breakables. That long club in the boy's room should be gone as well."

"Yes my Lord Urgess." His aide said, "Will there be anything else?"

"For now, Valegen, we should make ready for the emotional scenes to come; after all, when you ruin someone's life, they're bound to be angry."

Michael and Ralton came back to the apartment in two hours.

"That pizza was the bomb, dad," commented Ralt.

"Yeah, it was. I feel better when I've had something to eat." Michael replied, "Especially when I've had the kind of day I've had today."

As the pair came to the door, Ralt noticed the light under the door. "Dad, you turned off the lights, right?"

"Yeah, I did." Michael said suspiciously. "Kid, get back to the end of the hall. I'm gonna check this mess out." He pulled the studded gloves back on. Carefully, he slipped the key into the lock and was about to turn the key when the door opened.

A young pleasant looking man stood there with a warm friendly smile; he stood six foot two and had sharp distinctive features. "Good evening, sir, would you please come in?"

Michael stared at him, confused. Why was a stranger inviting him into his own apartment?

"If you and your son would please come in. You are in no danger."

Michael motioned Ralton to his side. "Yeah right…and the St. Thomas Bridge is for sale."

"Why do I think we're going to die?" asked Ralt apprehensively as they cautiously stepped into the living room.

The stranger dropped to Ralton's level. "You have no need to fear us young Ralton," the man smiled, "there is so much for you to learn; I am called Valegen."

Ralt pulled back as he saw the pointed ears. He looked at his father, ran a hand on his own ear. "Dad!"

Michael moved Ralt away from the man. "I don't care if you're Little Miss Muffet, what the fuck are you doing in my home?" This Valegen was part of the answer to what was happening to him.

"If I may take your coats?" Valegen asked noticing the rising anger in Michael's voice. Father and son gave up their coats. "My lord awaits you."

"I hope he's awaiting an ass kicking." Michael's voice was ice.

"Dad, the furniture's been changed." Ralt said as they entered the living room from the short hall.

"You are observant, Ralton." Valegen said. He looked at Michael who really didn't want to hear it.

"You are justifiably proud of him." A butter smooth voice came from one of the new wing back chairs arranged in a semi-circle in the living room. In one of them sat a man with dark red hair, the same type of sharp cheekbones only with a broken nose over a thin hard line of a mouth barely softened by the smile of welcome he wore. "I rather like these chairs, they are primitive but comfortable." He gestured to the chairs that were opposite of him. Michael and Ralton took them with great apprehension.

"Who the hell are you and what are you doing in my apartment?" Michael demanded.

"We are your people, Michael John Stone. Why we are here is simple; your father needs you." The man said.

"WHO THE HELL ARE YOU?!" Michael shouted as he jumped to his feet. A light came on in his eyes as he looked at the two strangers. He was starting to make sense of it now. They had to be behind what was happening to him even if he wasn't sure. Out of the corner of his eyes to his right, he saw two men in black step forward. Being no fool, Michael stepped back to his chair.

The stranger said. "I suggest you keep it quiet. Your neighbors will wonder what's happening to you and may call the police."

"Not in this hood." Michael said.

The man smiled knowingly. "You are quite right. They would not call, not over an argument. As I said; your father,"

"My father is dead you son of a bitch!" Michael snarled. "My mother saw him drown before I was born!"

"My mother was a good woman and you will not call

the queen mother a bitch again. Do you understand me? You father didn't drown, I was sent to collect him and bring him back home." The man said coldly.

"Bullshit!" Michael said. "There were three witnesses that day on the boat. Are you calling them liars?"

"No. I am saying they did not see what they thought they saw." The man said, looking Michael directly in the eyes. "His father wanted him back and he wanted him before he got further involved with your mother. It would not do to have an alien for a prince's wife. It would have upset the plans already set for him."

"So you let my mom think he drowned to keep him from marrying her? That's just wrong!" Michael said furiously. "Do you know what you put her through?"

"Yes I do. She did what she set out to do even with children, becoming a lawyer. It was a great tragedy when she died." The man said. The man's face was pained. "Once I found out her goals, I admired her. Not even a bastard son could stop her. You father did not leave her un-provided for. There was a fund to make sure she made it through college and see to your needs."

"I know about the money."

"Then you should be glad about it. After all, it was some of that money that allowed you to get Ralton into the world. Your executor was quite upset about that."

"He didn't let me have any more after that. He thought it was crazy to do that for an unborn child." Michael said. He stared at him. "How do you know about that? Not even my aunt knows about that money! There was more than what I paid Ralt's mother. I couldn't get to it until I hit twenty-one. When I did, I found out he was gone and I couldn't track him down." Michael felt a chill.

The man looked at him with sympathy. "He was ordered back home to Aboria. Unfortunately, we didn't get around to finding a replacement for him. By the time we did get someone, you were working. You didn't need our money."

Michael felt a hole in his stomach. Ralt looked at his father with confusion. "I don't get it. Why didn't you just tell us you were here all this time?"

The man smiled. He genuinely liked Ralton. "Because young Ralton, we had to figure out a way to get you. It took time."

"How long?" asked Ralt.

"A year. We had to figure out a way to make sure you would come with us."

Ralton gave one of those kid looks that said he was full of it. "You could figure it out in a few days."

"Very well. We took an extended vacation." Valegen smiled at being caught. His lordship gave him a sour eye. "That much is true, my lord. After all, we did see quite a few of the sights. I will admit to a taste for jazz."

"Valegen, you're telling tales."

"But not out of school." Valegen said. "My Lord Urgess, we should at least admit we needed to know what he was about. That did take time."

"What did he call you?" asked Ralt.

"Urgess. It is my name. Urgess Petron." The man said. "Urgess would translate to 'knight' in your language."

"In any case my lords we have a big day tomorrow." Valegen said. "Please understand lord Michael. What we do is for the best. You father has need of you. His people need you even if they don't know it yet. Please understand me when I say if there had been another way we would have done it."

"Tell that to my fucked reputation and my bank accounts." Michael said.

"Trust me when I say that you will have more at your disposal than you ever had." Urgess told him. "I suggest you get some rest. Valegen is right, you have a big day tomorrow." He stood and went to the closet.

Curious, Ralton followed him and looked in. "No way!" In the closet was the tesseract. In his wildest dreams he could not imagine there would be something like this in here. There were people moving around and doing things and working at desks and calling out things in a language he did not, could not know. Ralt's eyes were as big as saucers as he took it all in. Like Urgess and Valegen and he and his father, they all had pointed ears. For once in his life, Ralt felt like he belonged.

"Dad, you gotta see this!" Ralt said.

Michael joined him at the door and looked at the scene in astonishment. "Damn!" His voice very small, he stepped further into the tesseract. He looked at it slowly. "All this in here. We would have never known."

Valegen came to stand beside the father and son. "In truth, it is a small one. We felt we wouldn't need a large one since we didn't need a large crew." He looked at Michael. "It is very much like one of your stories."

"Yeah, it is." Michael shook his head. "I never expected to see anything like it in my life." He looked at Valegen. "You've read my stories?"

"Yes, we have. You know, the engineering is easy enough, and we know how to do it." Urgess said. "We created a stable tesseract address system and a stable tesseract."

"That goes without saying." Michael said as he ran his hand over a console's top. "This is stuff made from dreams."

Ralt watched a woman with a stylus draw an arc around some objects on the screen. He didn't know what she was doing, but it looked cool. He walked around the room looking at everything. Suddenly, he was living in a science fiction world for real. The personnel watched Ralt with indulgence. They knew the boy was completely fascinated by what he saw.

"Wow," Ralt breathed softly. "Wow."

"Do you wish to see what I see?" one of the technicians asked Ralt. The boy nodded yes. The tech stood and allowed Ralt in his seat. He put the goggles he wore on the boy and allowed him to see the multicolored scans of the sun he was watching.

"Whoa!" Ralt gasped as the scene danced in front of his eyes. "This is too awesome!"

The tech smiled at his companions. They knew exactly what Ralt meant since they felt the same way when they first looked through the goggles. The boy most likely never saw anything like it. They also knew that what lay ahead of him was far more impressive than this.

"My Lord, young Master, I suggest sleep. Tomorrow is a big day for you. I think you will want to be at your best for it." Valegen said.

Ralt reluctantly removed the goggles. He knew the tech had to get back to work. Michael and Ralton followed Valegen out. Ralt found new pajamas laid out for him. Michael found the same. First Ralt was settled in for the night. Michael went into the other bedroom.

Michael looked at his clock on the table. "Eleven o'clock. I am glad this day is over."

"But a new one tomorrow and the start of a new life," Valegen said.

"Did it ever occur to you I wasn't done with the current one yet?" asked Michael as he pulled off his shirt. "Then again, you've been in my closet for a year. Lord only knows what kind of wackos you've got where you come from." He stripped down to his shorts. Valegen realized he was going to sleep in the nude. He had to admit he admired Michael's lean muscular form. "You like living in someone else's closet or do you have claustrophobia?"

"A research team was assigned to you a year ago; we came here six months later to do the final work. We had to know where you were vulnerable, of course, in order to make sure you would come with us. If there was any other way, we would have found it." Valegen said.

"Still, you didn't leave me the option of refusal. Very neat." Michael said.

"We have read your stories, examined your drawings, listened to your music. You are beyond talented. You are what we are looking for." Valegen said. "Aren't you nervous with me in here?"

Michael chuckled. "You've been in my closet for a year. You've probably sent back some spectacular photos. Now you want to get nervous?" He slipped the shorts off. "Here's the real deal. Enjoy the view. Goodnight." He climbed into bed and pulled the covers over himself. "Turn the light off, will you?" he yawned, "Thanks."

Valegen watched as Michael turned on his side. Then he heard snoring. Valegen hit the light switch and left closing the door. "Remarkable! This will be interesting."

CHAPTER TWO

BENDING THE DIME

The next morning Michael and Ralton woke and found a set of clothes laid out for them and a well-made breakfast ready. While they ate, Urgess and Valegen told them what was in store.

"Today will be a shopping spree so you may get things you have always wanted." Urgess said. He smiled. "Last night you asked us who we were. As I said, we are your people. Your father is from our home world, Aboria. You notice we have many features in common," He indicated the pointed ears, "while it is true there are fairing races with pointed ears, you're special. Your father is our king."

Michael dropped the spoon he held, snorted derisively and then laughed out loud.

Urgess held his next thought and then said. "We find ourselves needing you. It will all be explained to you when you meet him."

"I can't wait to meet daddy dearest." Michael said.

"I have no doubt of that." Urgess replied noticing the

anger at the edges of Michael's voice. "Valegen will take you shopping. I'm sure there are more than a few things you have always wanted like mementos of Terra. Today you can get them."

"Right," Michael held his verbal fire. Urgess and Valegen knew they weren't whom Michael wanted. "Let's cruise for a while. After all, the really good shops don't open until ten o'clock." He got up and stretched and went to clean up.

Ralton finished his plate and watched as Urgess stood up and went to his "room". Valegen shook his head sadly. Ralton caught his expression. "What's the matter?"

"This is not the way I would have done this," Valegen mused.

"What do you mean?" asked Ralton.

"It seems our arrogance has betrayed us again." Valegen knew he shouldn't speak of these things to the ten-year-old. It had to be said. "Have you ever noticed how some people think they are so far superior that they may do what they want to others? It does not speak well of us when we do not think of how we affect others."

Ralt put his spoon down. "You mean they don't respect others?"

"Exactly. We did not respect your father or you. We have disrupted your lives for our needs. We may end up botching this. I am pleased it is not my decision to make."

Ralt shrugged his shoulders. "It sounds like somebody

goofed."

Valegen smiled. "I did think you were bright."

"Yeah, well, I'm glad I'm not an adult yet," said Ralt.

Valegen touched Ralton's hair marveling at the soft thickness. "Do yourself a favor, Ralton,"

"What's that?"

"Don't grow up too fast. Savor this time you've got. There will be time enough later for adult worries." Valegen smiled as he stood from the table. "We have a busy day ahead of us. I suggest you get cleaned up."

"Okay." Ralt swallowed the last spoonful of oatmeal and fruit, hopped off his chair and then headed for the bathroom.

Valegen knew he genuinely liked the father and son. This made what they did even harder. He like Urgess understood one thing after more than a year of observation Michael was made of stern stuff. Then again Valegen thought that may be just what was needed. He knew Michael didn't like the way this was handled, and he was furious. Whatever toys and things they bought today meant nothing. Michael would never, if he could help it, be a victim. Valegen chuckled. Yes, Michael was just what they needed.

"Take good care of them, Valegen." Urgess said to his aide as Michael, Ralton and Valegen got into the rental limo.

"Of course I shall, my lord." Valegen said as he settled in for the ride. "I'm sure this will be fun."

"Spending someone else's money always is. Enjoy your

selves. I've some work to finish, that's why I'm not going with you." Urgess told them.

"Well, gosh darn the luck!" Michael said in the sappiest voice he could manage. "Give us all a break. I figure you have to report in since you have your objective."

"In one of my preliminary reports, I said you were quite intelligent. I'd hate to have to revise that to asshole." Urgess stood away from the car and slapped its fender. Ralt doubled over in laughter. Valegen struggled to keep a straight face. Michael had a sheepish expression as the limo pulled smoothly away from the curb.

Urgess shook his head sadly as he went back inside to the stares of the neighbors. Once inside, he went into the tesseract room and sat down at a console, slipped on a headphone/microphone and spoke. "This is Urgess Alm Petron, code white. I have made contact with the half-breed and his son. Yes, yes, we will be ready in two Terran weeks. I cannot say he will calm down. You have threatened his son! My brother, this one has fire and you will be burned! He sighed. "The boy is about nine or ten Terran years old, quite bright and perceptive. From all of our interviews we have conducted, he worked hard for his dream job even with a child in tow. My lord, destroying him was not pleasant. I do believe he will hold a grudge. Were I you, I would be careful. I am not worried about me, he is not angry with me. Your will be done, Majesty, but I don't think it will be the way you want it."

Urgess listened closely and then replied. "I fear we have made a mistake in how we did it. I believe we brought some long buried feelings to surface. As I said, brother, your will be done."

Urgess pulled the headphones off. "Thail, you ass. I hope the boy drops you like a rock. You will have deserved it."

In the limo Valegen asked "what are your first purchases my lords?"

Ralton spoke up; "How about a blu-ray player dad? You always wanted one!"

Michael smiled. "Video it is. Son I like your style." He knocked on the partition glass. "Driver, do you know where Ken Crane's is in West Los Angeles?"

The driver nodded.

"Good," Michael said, "We'll go to Rogersound after that. I always wanted to see if they have the selection they say they do."

"You can afford it now." Valegen told him.

All fell silent. Valegen recalled the conversation with Urgess.

"A year of following him and his son my lord," Valegen massaged Urgess' back. "Michael has earned the life that he can make for himself. To destroy him is wrong."

"Don't I know it my dear one? I don't like it any more than you do. However, after two failures, Thail is determined to get this right. You know how it was with Jatis and Brok." Urgess sighed as Valegen kneaded a tight spot. "He's got twenty bastards. He should know by now that he can't just do anything to any of them."

"Poor Jatis and Brok. They didn't work out so well, did they?" asked Valegen. "With poor Brok in a coma for six years and Jatis taking refuge in drugs, it must hurt him greatly."

"Jatis did that to himself. He couldn't take the pressure." Urgess said. "He was only a boy, much younger than Michael."

"Do you think Michael can take the pressure?" asked Valegen.

Urgess gave a hearty laugh. "What do you think?"

Valegen sat upright and wiped his hands on a hot towel. "I think if the King keeps out of the way, he may get what he wants. Perhaps even more than he expected." He applied more oil to his hands and bent back to massaging Urgess. "I still don't think its Michael's problem to deal with."

"I agree." Urgess gave a soft moan as his muscles began to relax. "It seems to me that Thail should give as much as he is asking. You know, I think Michael will take it out of Thail for not coming here himself. There are a lot of issues that need to be dealt with. I don't think my brother gets it. Michael's anger might be taken out of his father's hide. I can't wait to see it!" He ran his hand along Valegen's inner thigh and gripped his manhood and sighed. "Why don't you give me a full body massage. I'm sure your hands are tired."

"Not yet my love," Valegen said as he slid next to Urgess in the bed.

"Ken Crane's, my lords," The driver said as they pulled into the parking lot of the electronics store.

"Right," Valegen said, "are we ready to shop?"

"Yeah!" Ralt said as he allowed the driver to open the door.

"I think so." Michael said as he got out. "You got the big dime, and this is one of many toy chests. Ready to see your dime bent?"

Valegen gave him an indulgent smile. "If you think you're up to the task. Are you ready to go inside?"

"You make it sound like you have a mark for us to hit." Michael said as they entered the store.

"If you must know it is two hundred fifty thousand American." Valegen informed him.

Michael looked at him. "So where did you get the money?"

"Let's just say your account is full and leave it at that." Valegen said as he made his way to a display. "We also have some credit cards that will be paid off the moment you purchase something."

"You got that much jack in the box?" asked Michael.

"Yes." Valegen said. "You should see the size of the box."

Michael's eye went wide with disbelief. "Damn, Sam! We got to spend your money."

A pleasant looking sales woman greeted the two while they stood in the middle of the store getting their bearings. "Good morning, how may I help you?"

Michael spotted her name tag. "Good morning Marge." They shook hands. He pointed to Ralt. "Do you see that young blood over there looking over the blu-ray players? That's my son. In two days it will be his birthday. I promised him he could have a flat screen television and blu-ray for his room, and this year I can afford to spoil him rotten. I'd like it if you would help him pick out his present. I figure, this sort of thing will only happen once."

Marge said "it sounds like you will be paying for a lot this year."

Michael smiled. "You don't know how much I've paid already." Valegen gave Michael a shot in the ribs with his elbow. Michael rubbed the spot. "What was that for?"

"Gauche crypticness," Valegen returned. "I want to check out their plasma units."

"Wait a minute. Call me slow, call me stupid, but don't you guys have major video systems of your own? Our stuff isn't even a blip on your radar," said Michael as they made their way to the display of thin plasma unit televisions.

"For your information you can tell a lot about a people with how they entertain themselves. Besides it is easier to do a retrofit. This isn't for your benefit alone." Valegen explained. "In any case, I must admit to a great love of your animation films. We have them, but yours has so much more to them, more life. I also like the James Bond films."

At that Michael had to stuff his fist into his mouth to stifle the laughter.

"They're good fun movies! What's so strange about that?" Valegen defended himself.

It took Michael a while to finally calm down.

"For you information, I also like the blues and the music of the British Invasion." Valegen told the still gasping Michael. "Urgess likes American Standards and jazz."

Michael held up a hand as he gasped for breath. "It's cool, it's all good. I'm just surprised, that's all." He turned to see Ralt taking a stack of DVD and blu-ray DVD to the counter. There were two blu-ray DVD players and Michael heard Marge talking about the plasma screen TV that was being brought out of the back room.

Michael looked at Valegen. "I think the boy is ahead of us."

"You think we should catch up?" asked Valegen.

"Sounds like a plan." Michael and Valegen looked over the selection and made their buys. Valegen handed Michael an American Express card with his name on it. "Platinum, very nice."

Michael looked at Valegen slightly cockeyed.

"We know you know you don't like to think about money all the time." Valegen said. "You just like to make sure you can pay for everything."

"True," Michael said nonplussed, "I just guess it's the

modesty." He handed the card over and watched, as the purchases were totaled. Fifty-two thousand, nine hundred and seventy dollars at this store. "That's just with three of everything."

"It's not just for your benefit alone," Valegen told him, "it allows us to gauge where your people are. You can tell a lot about a people by watching how they play."

"That's why we got five of everything," said Ralt.

"Yes, only one of what we brought will go to Urgess or I, the rest will go to our archives," explained Valegen. "Besides, there is a lot of your entertainment I like."

"Can't buy me love, everybody tells me so," Michael sang. "No, no, no."

"Very funny my lord," Valegen whispered in the grinning Michael's ear. Valegen gave the store an address to take the goods to and led father and son out to the car. Ralt had a portable DVD player and several movies he would watch between stores. Valegen and Michael watched Ralt as he enjoyed his new toy.

"Where next?" asked Valegen.

"Let me ask you something first. When did I get the card?" asked Michael turning it over in his fingers.

"We set it up six months ago. It has a great credit rating. We had to make sure that it was ready for you," replied Valegen.

"How convenient, make sure the velvet cage is well lined." quipped Michael.

"If you insist, yes. Of course, the equipment will be modified," Valegen saw the look on Michael's face, "we've done a good job on you." He made sure he said it, not Michael.

Tower Records was next in West Hollywood along with every video and record store in the area. Valegen made sure that everything went to the address. They had several people in a pair of vans waiting to take everything they bought.

Bookstores were next. Trash and time honored were put into a library of some fifteen thousand titles. They knew they got multiples sometimes, but it was worth it. Valegen produced several other credit cards so the one they were using didn't run too high. Michael thought it was silly since he now knew they had the money to cover everything.

They hit computer stores next including the new Apple store in the Grove at Farmer's Market.

"Guitar Center, driver." Michael turned to Valegen, "your dime is about to be seriously hurt Val."

"Let me guess. You are about to completely take the store with you." Valegen smirked. "It is not as if you haven't tried already."

"I've got my music Jones up. There are things in there I have only dreamed about." Michael said.

"In that case let's have lunch. We need to give the crews time to take the other purchases to the storage." Valegen said.

"You mean we bought that much stuff?" asked Ralt.

"Dear boy, I doubt we have truly gotten everything your

father has ever wanted." Valegen said. "As a matter of fact I'm surprised you haven't gone to the places where you can get video equipment."

"That's afterward." Michael said.

"Forgive me, I didn't know." Valegen smiled.

"You are such a liar!" Michael said. "You know full well I'm into all things motion picture. It's been my biggest dream to direct film and television. Hell, I was working a project after work."

"You mean the "Mister Beaujay" project?" asked Valegen.

"Dad based that on a story he wrote when I was little. He couldn't afford books for me, so he wrote his own. I think there's about ten of them." Ralt said as they came to the Guitar Center.

"Actually, there are twelve. I know I looked." Valegen told him.

"You read them all?" asked Ralt as he turned the DVD player off.

"My favorite is 'Mister Beaujay and the Great Steamship of the Air'. The fact that the drawings look like you and your father helped a lot." Valegen winked. "Did you do that so that there was an adventure story that had a black male in the lead and a black child as the sidekick?"

Michael smiled. "Yeah, I wanted something Ralt and I could relate to. I wanted him to see that we were capable of great inventiveness like everyone else."

"I like the part where the steamship lifts off for the first time and the great race with the jealous rival around the world." Valegen enthused. "Trust me when I say this. Those stories are going to be published when we get to Aboria. They are too much fun not to be. The drawings will have to be copied. The books you made are a little ratty and falling apart."

"You are kidding, right?" asked Michael.

"No, I'm not. Those books will be a hit." Valegen said as they got out the car.

The three of them stood outside of the building, Michael thought of all the times he came in this place and made a wishing shopping list. All the things he wanted. All the instruments. He owned a used Fender electric piano and some inexpensive electric guitars and basses. The drum set was worn and needed new heads. There was a pair of low-end synthesizers and now he was about to put that wish list to sleep.

Valegen saw it. He knew the young man next to him had big dreams and now those dreams were real.

Michael reached into his pocket. Behind him the two crews Valegen hired pulled into the lot and parked behind him. They stood behind him and one of them saw the list on the tattered piece of paper Michael kept in his wallet. One item was crossed off. He reached in his pocket and pulled out a pen. He looked at his list again and smiled. "Gentle people," he said, "we are about to put the dime in traction." They went inside. Their party was spotted and a young man with a set of three earrings in on ear and five in the other came up to them. Michael saw the extensive tattoos on his arms. The young man whose name tag said "Gary" asked; "can I help you with anything?"

"Have you got the afternoon?" Michael asked.

"Well, yeah. I am here to help." Gary replied.

"Gary, my brother, we are here to do serious damage to your stock. Do you still have that Mini-Moog?" asked Michael.

"Yeah, we do. We get one in every so often." answered Gary. He could see a major sale in Michael's eyes. It was the kind of look Gary had in his own eyes when he could afford something important to him.

"Ralton?" asked Michael.

"Yes, dad?" replied his son.

"Pick out the basses you like. I'm in keyboards." Michael told his son. Michael strode into the keyboards section of the store stopping to survey the lot. He knew what he wanted, knowing the drought was over.

Valegen and Ralt hung back with Gary, who look at the two and asked, "Is he serious?"

"Yes," Valegen said, "and that scares me!" He turned to Ralton. "shall we pick out your instruments?"

"Yes." Ralt answered. "Gary, I think you should go with my dad, he may hurt somebody." Suddenly, there was a wicked rendition of Stop! In the Name of Love from the keyboard room along with an impassioned vocal.

"I didn't know you father could play that well." Valegen said. "He really means it!"

"Well, when you've been playing on crappy instruments for as long as he has, you get real good to make up for it." Ralt said. "Dad has been promising himself something like this for a long time. I'm glad it's happening."

"Amazingly enough, so am I." Valegen said as he followed Ralt into the guitar section.

Another two hours and they were out of the store. Virtually everything Michael wanted he got including things to help him on video projects. He supposed there were far more advanced versions of the same thing where they were going, but at least, he now finished off his list. They also went to Goodman's Music on Cahuenga Boulevard and bought what they had as well.

They went to Samy's Camera on Fairfax and bought all the video equipment they had; they also hit the other camera stores Michael knew of and bought what they had as well; all of his video dreams were fulfilled.

All in all, it was eight o'clock when they finally slowed down and saw they had time enough for dinner before they went home. Ralt fingered his new Fender bass and Michael ran riffs on his Stratocaster guitar. Michael was proud he taught himself and then Ralt how to play. It made for a sweet noise in the back of the limo as they rode to a small restaurant for dinner.

The driver followed them in and took a table opposite them and had them clearly covered.

"The driver is one of yours, right?" Michael asked.

"Yes. He had been trained to deal with Los Angeles traffic." Valegen said.

"I guess I am important to you. You want to make sure you don't lose me before we get to this Aboria." Michael lifted a fork full of mashed potatoes to his mouth. He'd get to the roast beef and green beans next.

Valegen cut into his New York strip steak with a baked potato and green beans; Ralt had the t-bone even though he knew he'd never finish it.

"You don't know how important you are. Our people need you." Valegen told him and then lifted a forkful of food to his mouth.

"Yeah, I guess. Michael said. "If I'm so important, why didn't my father come down here and get me himself? Hell, all he had to do was tell me who he was. I'd drop everything and take off with him."

Valegen looked down at his plate. "We were afraid you wouldn't come. We wanted to make sure you would leave the planet."

"Would you have left Ralt?" asked Michael.

"Would you kill us if we did?" asked Valegen.

"Yeah, I would."

"Then we're not as stupid as you thought." Valegen said as he began on another piece of his excellent steak. He swallowed. "Look. Michael, if it makes you feel any better, we simply wanted to make sure that you would come. We had to make sure you had no real ties to keep you here. Ralton is too powerful an inducement to make sure we got it right. You would have to come if we simply took the boy. Not being complete fools, we made sure Ralt was included." He cut another piece. "You never deny the parent his child. That would have brought a madness I don't think any of us would survive."

"But you still screwed me over. That's not going to stop hurting for a while." Michael said.

"I know." Valegen sighed. "Sometimes we forget John, that we don't have all the answers, nor do we know all the questions. Many people are in the house. That's your greater family and they didn't want to do this. My problem is, was there another way? If we had known of your desires that would have been the way to you. I think our research was incomplete."

"No kidding!" Michael said. "Look, this thing, whatever it is, is going to affect Ralt too." Michael spoke firmly. He kept the harshness out of his voice. He was beginning to like Valegen. "What you did was flat out wrong. You simply had no right to do that. I had a life, damn it all! What gives you the right to destroy it?"

"There is a world that has lost its way. It needs to reconcile with some of its children. You are one of the children made and abandoned by their fathers. They need to learn to respect you." Valegen's voice was quiet. "We haven't done that, have we? Our arrogance, our pride." He slammed his fists on the table making Ralt and his father jump. "We keep doing it wrong, wrong, wrong!" He hung his head and then broke into unexpected tears. "We have done you wrong. All the shit we've bought is nothing to what we have done to you." He put his face in his hands and shook with rage and grief and the other patrons watched as he sobbed into his hands. He looked at Michael as if seeing him for the first time. "I'm sorry, John. We are so very wrong. There is nothing in my power I can do about it." He hung his head down again.

Michael could see that Valegen had no idea what to do or say. He silently wept and Ralt watched as he father placed a hand on the guilt wracked man's shoulder and said "I don't blame you. You're not responsible for what happened."

"I played a part in it, John. I am as responsible as anyone in this." Valegen said. Michael relieved him of the responsibility. Still he felt it no matter what Michael said.

"Valegen, no matter what, you've been pretty nice about all of this." Michael said. "Hell, you've given me and Ralt one of the best days we've ever had. Something like this can't come from someone who is a total bastard. So, maybe there is something good in your people. Maybe you're not seeing it."

"Maybe I see them all too well, John. It hurts to see your people in a pain of their own making." Valegen said as he wiped his face with the hot towel the waitress brought him. "I'm sorry. I'm acting like an infant."

"Babies are more honest than adults anyway." Ralt said.

"He's right you know." Michael said. "Now tell me about my father's people."

41

CHAPTER THREE

TRUTH AND DARES

"I'm not sure if I should do that here." Valegen said.

Ralt sat up. "I wouldn't mind."

"You heard him." Michael said.

"I have a near complete breakdown and you want to hear about your father's people." Valegen said. "Have you no mercy?"

"I have plenty of mercy." Michael said. "I think you owe me."

Valegen looked away. He wasn't really sure what to say. This was not the best place to say what he had to say. Then again, the restaurant was perfect. No one else was really listening.

"All right," Valegen began "my world is called Aboria. We of course are Aborians. Your father, our king, is called Thail Marius Petron." He smiled. "In fact, your name Stone and Petron means the same thing. Twenty-nine years ago, your father came to this world. To be honest he was running away from his duties and himself. He really didn't want to be king. He didn't want to be tied to the throne nor did he want the responsibility. I don't blame him. That crown can be so damned heavy.

Any way, he met your mother and amazingly enough, they fell in love even though your mother never knew this. He was betrothed to his queen. We had an idea he may have impregnated her. Later reports proved this to be true."

"You had people watching my mother?" asked an incredulous Michael.

"Yes. Once you were born, we had a watch placed on you to insure your safety in case we might need you." He saw the skeptical looks on both their faces. "That's what I was told. I do know one thing. The queen kept notes on all of his children."

"All of his children? How many children did he have?" asked Michael.

"Outside of the marriage? He had, including you, twenty children. Within the marriage, ten children."

"You're kidding, right?" asked Ralt. "He had that many girlfriends?"

"Damn! The boy's seed works!" Michael said.

"It worked quite well. He of course couldn't know all of them well." Valegen continued. "As I said, the queen kept records on the entire group of out of wedlock children. She also made contact with the mothers and made sure they were taken care of."

"Why would she do that?" asked Ralt. "I mean these

weren't her kids, right?"

Valegen smiled. "She thought of the women as a sisterhood, a sisterhood of the betrayed. The trouble was it was an old, old, story. We make the children, but we don't acknowledge them. Therein is our biggest mistake. We keep making enemies we don't need." He took a drink from the wine and then continued. "The queen told him she would suffer no more women in his life. If he wanted to have another woman he would have to stick with what he knew. The women who bore his children."

"Didn't it bother her that she would be sharing him with those other women?" asked Ralt. "I mean, he was her husband!"

Valegen looked at Michael. "How does he know these things?"

"You have seen the soap operas we have here?" asked Michael. "It's total schooling in all the lurid arts."

Valegen shook his head in amazement. "I didn't pay attention to them. In any case, he actually stopped playing around and settled down to being the king and a husband. His wife made sure that he was as happy as he could be." He saw the look on Ralt's face. "Understand something, she likes being queen. She will not trade that for anything. She does love him, hard as that is."

"Y'all messed up." Ralt said. "If the man made all these children, why doesn't he know them?"

"The fact is I don't think any man can really know all

his children as well as he could." Valegen told them. "The king tries." he shook his head sadly.

"What's my part in all this?" asked Michael asked.

Sighing again, Valegen continued. "John, thirty percent of our population is mixed-blood. That is part of the problem. We have been in space a long time. The children of many a dalliance had one thing in common, their fathers refused to and did not acknowledge them. We have written bad laws against them; we have abandoned our honor, we have lost our way with them." He drained his wine and filled the glass again. A second thought crossed his mind but he kept the glass at hand.

"Too many people both half-breed and full-blood live in the worst kind of poverty, without hope. John, from everything we've learned, you never gave up hope. Even at your lowest point, you never stopped believing. You kept your faith, you kept trying." He stared at Michael. "You have what we lack, the courage to do the right thing."

"Was anyone else tried before?" asked Michael.

Valegen nodded. "Two of your brothers were tried. Jatis and Brok. Our problem was we tried to make them something they weren't, and they paid for it. If the king is smart, he will leave you be who you are and let you grow into the role. If we are wise, you will get the ancestri, your blood knowledge. In that you will have a strength the others lacked, the power to do what needs to be done."

"I'm no messiah." Michael said.

"Yet that is what we are trying to make you, isn't it?" Valegen said. "Yet that may be what saves you. I don't think Aboria is worth it. I pray we can keep you whole."

"Did they die?" asked Ralt.

"For all the good they did, they may as well have died. I don't want to see a repeat, not again." Valegen said grimly.

"Look, Valegen, I won't tell Urgess we talked about the mess I'm headed for, okay?" Michael said.

"It won't matter, my lord knows me well enough to know we did talk." Valegen said.

"I guess so. I saw how fond you are of each other." Michael said.

"That much is obvious? Our relationship goes back a bit. He may know me better than my mother." Valegen admitted.

Michael turned to Ralt. "Are you ready?"

"I got to go to the bathroom." Ralt jumped off his chair and went to the bathroom.

"Why is it called a bathroom if you can't take a bath?" asked Valegen.

Michael broke up laughing.

"It's an honest question!"

"I just never thought of it!" replied Michael after he stifled an embarrassing snort.

Ralt returned from the bathroom. "I'm ready."

They paid their check and then left.

By the time they got to the apartment, Valegen had been silent the entire ride. Apparently, Valegen was still feeling something. Even the driver noticed it.

"You okay Valegen?" asked Michael as they got out of the limo.

"I won't be all right for a while. I still feel bad about all of this." Valegen told him. He saw Ralt pulling the bass out with him. "You can leave it, Hovak will get that."

Ralt left the instrument in the car and joined his elders with a worried look on his face. Valegen looked as if he would have a complete breakdown, this time worse than in the restaurant. Michael saw it too. He grabbed Valegen by the shoulders. "Damn it, Val, get out of it! It's done and you can't change it! Whatever we have to go through, we will go through it and deal with it!" Valegen looked away. Michael turned his face back to him and stared him in the eyes. "If you weren't good at what you do, Urgess wouldn't have you, and you know it!" He let go of the shoulders as Valegen stared at him. The half-breed was not going in the apartment until he pulled himself together. "You knew what you were doing the minute you set out to get me." He pointed to the driver. "Hell, even Hovak knew what was up! So don't give me the regret now." Michael could see that Valegen was starting to see what he meant. "You've handled the heat so far. Don't ever forget that you can handle it and don't ever show the regret." He got closer. "If you like me and Ralt, thank you. But do your job."

Valegen was shocked. Michael accepted what was happening to him, why couldn't he? He knew why. He was afraid for the father and son, afraid his world would eat them alive. Why this fear would hit him so hard was beyond him. He looked away from Michael then back at him. "I'm sorry, John. I'm so very sorry."

"We both know that. Now we got to do what we got to do." Michael turned on his heel and went up the stairs to his apartment.

At the top of the stairs Ralt spotted him first.

"Come on, move it Ralt." Michael told his son.

"Dad, Godzilla's landed."

Michael saw him, and saw what Ralt meant. The man at the top of the stairs had a heavily sculpted face with a scar over his right eye. The natural eye was replaced with an artificial eye that glowed red from the socket and both the eyes regarded the group coming up the stairs coldly. To Ralt, the man was a living daemon, coldly surveying its next meal. Michael's reaction was almost as bad. Worse, the man was staring directly at him with the coldness in his eyes intensifying if that was possible. "Who the hell is that?!" He asked Valegen.

"That is Gherrict, another uncle of yours. If he's here, you're getting the ancestri here on Earth. A word of caution. He doesn't have a sense of humor." Valegen was sympathetic.

They finished the climb of the stairs. At the top, Ralt

tried to slip past Gherrict. The alien caught him by the arm. Michael moved to get to them, but Valegen stopped him. The voice was harsh and cold. "Do you fear me boy?"

Ralt nervously nodded yes.

"Know this. Unless you are foolish or do wrong in my presence, you have very little to fear." Gherrict softened his voice for Ralt. "What I have to show you is very special for you and your father. You will learn so much in the short time we have. It may frighten you. Do not be afraid, no harm will come to you." He cupped the boy's chin in his hand. "I do not lie to you." He stood and let the boy shoot into the apartment.

Gherrict's coldness returned to him. "Are you done with your foolishness, Valegen? I have need of them now."

Valegen could hardly keep the fear out of his voice. "Yes Lord Gherrict, they are ready for you. We are done for the time."

"Good. This will take one Terran week." Gherrict did not take his eyes off Michael as he spoke with Valegen. "You may have them back after that, albeit changed." He went inside.

Michael was visibly shaken. "That is one spooky son of a bitch." He hadn't met the person who could scare him like that before now.

"I most certainly agree with you." Valegen said as he followed Michael in the apartment.

The next morning, Gherrict woke Michael.

Michael looked at the bedside clock. He looked at Gherrict. "It's three in the morning. Do you know how early that is?" He pulled the covers back over his head.

Gherrict's eyes narrowed to slits as he grabbed the sleepy younger man and pulled him out of bed. Michael landed on the floor surprised. "Get up, boy! I am not your idiot father. You will not speak to me without respect and obedience! Is that understood? When I tell you to do something, I expect it done. Now get up!"

Michael sat on the floor not caring what Gherrict did. "Are you some kind of fool or what?!"

The huge man was having none of it and grabbed Michael by the hair and stood him up. "Don't give me trouble, boy!

"I am not a boy!" Michael got into Gherrict's face and stared into his eyes.

Gherrict locked his stare with him. "Are you one hundred and eight years of age?"

Michael stared back. Gherrict didn't look a day over forty. "No."

"Then you are a boy. Come along."

Michael hesitated. "I'm naked. Do you mind if I dress?"

"If you will notice, this is all I'm wearing." Gherrict threw him a male thong.

Michael saw what Gherrict wore. "The girls would love you in that.

"You are an ass, boy. Did you know that?" Gherrict was disgusted. "Put it on and come along."

"Do you always hold people in contempt or do you think your shit don't stink?" asked Michael.

"I am better than you. Don't forget it." Gherrict said as he left the room. Michael got the 'g' string on and then followed him out muttering "motherfucker."

Gherrict was standing at the front closet when Michael joined him. Gherrict regarded the younger man. He closed his eyes and took a deep breath, and then spoke. "What you are about to experience is most holy for those who achieve it. The ancestri allows you full knowledge of whom and what you are. It is…how do I put this for you? It is attainment of a glimpse into your soul. A recognition of all your strengths." He looked at Michael. "Even you should appreciate this. It is more than I can express in words." He opened a door into another "room" in the tesseract. It was dark in here. There was a flat metal bowl on legs with oil in it. Gherrict lit this and watched as the oil burned brightly illuminating the room.

"Look at me, boy. What do you see?" Gherrict asked.

Michael knew this was no time to be flippant; this mattered to Gherrict. Whatever was going to happen was happening. "You're wearing interlocking earrings with black stones and . . ."

"Say it!" Gherrict demanded.

"Your nipples and navel are pierced." Michael finished.

"Do you know why?"

"No."

Gherrict pointed to his left nipple. "Gheron world of my birth. The right is Abor. The navel is me."

Michael thought about it. He related it to a story he'd read about people who symbolized who they were with jewelry or tattoos. He noticed that the tattoos wove their way across his body and formed intriguing patterns on his body. "The copulation of two worlds resulting in you."

"Very good. Abor is in you, Michael, only you don't know it. You are half complete. You, whether you can say it or not, understand Terra. That is a given." There was a circle on the floor. Gherrict went to one side and sat down. Michael, not knowing what to do sat on the other side of it. "I am not your father who fucked his way across the galaxy. I am your teacher and you will respect me and obey me. Do you understand this? If I have to, I will beat you into the bloodiest pulp possible."

Michael saw the fire in Gherrict's eyes. He also saw the huge hands resting on the man's knees. "I understand." Michael said.

"Good. Let us begin." Gherrict said.

One week. That's all it took. By cutting Michael off from all outside influences, Gherrict was able to concentrate his effort and lessons and double them. He pushed Michael like he never was pushed before. He could do so since Michael was a fast learner and an intense student as Gherrict was a teacher. His estimation of Michael rose considerably.

That first day had Michael deep inside the ancestri as Gherrict explained what the ancestri were. Michael was nervous, and the lessons forced him to look deeper inside than he ever did. It made him nervous to see the great nexus of worlds, bright shining crossroads that led to every world that was. He could see the people that were connected to him, even if it was all theory to others, imaginings that took him away from his own doubts. Mikal could feel the connections going deeper than he ever thought they could.

At one point. Gherrict had Mikal spread his arms to his sides, palms up. Small glowing spheres hovered just above his palms, and Michael could feel power, real power, coursing through him.. As the sarcasm was gone, there was only truth revealed. What it meant to be a soulmage, what the ancestri meant, and where his place was in all of it. All of those, even the most primitive of beings were part of the lineage of his family. Now that family included all men, of two worlds.

There was shuddering new knowledge of his place in the universe, and it scared him. The responsibility of it!

Gherrict took him to a place where time slowed considerable. He trained him in martial arts just for the physical discipline.

The beauty of the stars washed over him.

Then he saw himself, and others on his world and was saddened. They were all made of the same star stuff. They were all the same dust and breath and gifts granted by the universe. He saw the same on the new world he was to go to, Aboria. He saw how crooked and bent out of shape, how lost people were. He didn't want the responsibility, even if he knew he could not walk away from it.

Again, Gherrict had him take the pose of a cross. This time, the spheres looked like Earth and Aboria, and he could feel the true power pulse through the spheres.

"They are yours, nephew. none can take them away from you.." Gherrict told him, Michael's body covered in sweat again.

Michael and Ralton even sang a deep healing song. But Ralt's voice was strong and pure and Michael could feel deep power in his son's song. "Ralton, you are blessed with a great power, all your own."

Gherrict taught Michael and Ralton through that deep and satisfying week.

"Very well done, nephew," Gherrict said after a particularly intense lesson. Once again, this lesson left Michael in the middle of the great nexus of worlds, leaving both men sweating profusely. "Assume the position." He and Michael slipped into the lotus. "What are the eight steps?"

"The eight steps are honor, duty, responsibility, kindness, forgiveness, compassion, courage and trust." Michael responded.

Gherrict smiled. He was doing more of that as Michael came to understand what was being taught. He touched fingertips together, brought them to his lips and then spoke. "Now we come to a most difficult part. All that you have learned leads to this. I know you are ready. Your hunger to learn is phenomenal."

Michael smiled. That much was true.

"As Valegen has told you, for far too long we have neglected all of our children, not just our half-breeds. I was the first half-breed in our house to be acknowledged by your grandfather Raniu Petron. He realized Aboria made many of these children and was failing them. Then it got worse. Three hundred years ago, laws were first passed to try and stop breeds from integrating into our society. There were miscegenation laws, laws blocking half-breeds from inheriting estates even if it were the parent's will. These and other ways were used to keep these unwanted children from truly integrating into our society."

Gherrict sighed. "Nephew, your father has sired some twenty children out of wedlock. He has ten by his queen. Thirty children total."

"The boy's tool is limber." commented Michael.

"I agree." Gherrict continued. "As you know, the queen tracked these other women down, became friends with them. However, two died leaving orphaned sons ripe for the picking."

"Jatis and Brok," spoke Michael.

"Yes. My mistake is that I did not give them what I am giving you. Like most others, I thought they would not need it. The worst mistake I could have ever made. Abor ate them alive. Brok is in a coma. He was put there by an extremist who did not believe he should be governor of a sector. Brok was ambushed as he was going to his office to begin a day's work." He shook his head sadly. "Jatis turned to drugs to keep the world at bay. He may as well be in a coma. I failed them by not acting in their best interest and giving them the ancestri before we gave them to Abor." He leaned forward. "The ancestri will be your edge, Michael. You know yourself in ways you have not imagined. Your father didn't want this to happen. However, his queen asked me to do this. She understood all that knowledge would be needed."

"Dang, behind his back!" Michael said. "Is he that clueless?"

"Your father is a proud and stubborn man. Even when he admits he's wrong he loathes to truly change." Gherrict told him.

Michael saw the heaviness in his uncle. "The Queen was willing to change, was willing to embrace these other women. Why couldn't he do the same?"

Gherrict shrugged. "If I could understand why Aborians could lay with so many people and leave them with children the fathers didn't want, I would. You know, your grandfather took pity on me and gave me the ancestri just as mother gave me Gheron. Father knew I wasn't the one. I could teach the one who could."

Michael buried his face in his hands and then leaned

back as frustration and a welling anger showed in his eyes. "I'll tell you what I told Valegen. I am no messiah."

"Nor should you be. Yet that is what we are asking you to do, be a messiah." Gherrict could feel the growing reluctance and pain from his nephew. He reached out with his soul to comfort Michael and steel him. "Jon, I call you Jon. Let me give you the ancestri, then you decide. If you say no, at least you will have your full self."

"Do I really have any choice?" asked Michael.

"You already know the answer to that, don't you?" replied Gherrict. The two looked at each other. Finally, Michael spoke.

"You've taken me this far. You might as well take me all the way."

Michael thought he saw pride in Gherrict's eyes. "My nephew, thank you. You are the most courageous man I know."

"Don't bet on it. One of my teachers used to say sometimes you have to eat shit and bark at the moon to get where you need to go." Michael said.

"This is not shit, Jon."

"Don't tell that to my mouth, Uncle."

Gherrict lit the brazier on the floor between them. The flame leaped, illuminating the room. He assumed the lotus again and Michael did the same. They both closed their eyes as Gherrict began to chant:

"Hear me, oh blood,

That flows through me
That is of my forefather's
That is of me
Begs to see thee,
Begs to learn from thee,
Hear me, oh blood
That flows through me!"

When Gherrict finished his chant, the room began to swirl from darkness to warm shimmering light. The swirls of light took form and voice.

"WHO CALLS?"

"Keep your head bowed until you are told to look, Michael." Gherrict whispered. He then raised his voice in humble supplication. "I call you, oh honored ones. My soul begs to hear thee."

"YOU ARE CALLED GHERRICT, CHILD."

"As I am called, honored ones." Gherrict said.

"WHY DO YOU CALL US, CHILD?"

"I bring before you one who may be able to heal our sick and grieving world."

"LET US SEE HIS FACE."

"We look up at the same time." Gherrict said; they did so and Michael opened his eyes slowly. "This one is called Michael John Stone. He brings with him new blood, a son of his own that has risen since his sixteenth year."

Suddenly, the ghostly forms took on solid shape, looking like every person, of all stripes and all colors from both worlds with glows around them, lifting him causing him to whisper "oh, my god." in a small voice. Suddenly, the nexus of two worlds was around him and he could feel the power coursing through him. Gherrict and Ralton were there and their bodies pulsed with power. But Michael and Ralt were side by side at the center point of the nexus, and the father and son could feel power, in the form of light and water flow through them again. It was the greatest love that made Michael fight for his son's life and choose to raise him. It was the connection that made father and son so powerful, because Michael did not run from the responsibility of being Ralton's parent.

"WE ARE NOT GODS MIKAL JON STON-PETRON! WE ARE OF YOU AND YOU ARE OF US!"

"WE REJOICE THAT YOU DID NOT RUN FROM BLOOD BUT DID ACCEPT IT AND LOVE IT ERE BIRTH!"

"OH SWEET JOY TO KNOW THAT HONOR AND LOVE HAS NOT DIED!"

"BE WELCOME, OH CHILD OF OURS! BE LOVED AND CHERISHED! BE IT KNOWN TO YOU WE SHALL NOT DESERT YOU IF YOU DO NOT DESERT YOURSELF!"

"HE IS THE ONE! HE IS WHOLE! HE IS THE

ONE!"

So solid now. They were holding him and touching him and it all went straight to his soul. It was celebratory, erotic, nourishing and healing. He could tell that hearts, minds and souls rejoiced that Mikal did not turn from his unborn son but chose to raise him with all the love and courage that he had.

When they set he and Ralton down, they was covered from head to foot in sweat. There was a fire in their eyes that matched Gherrict's. There was pride in his uncle's face. "You have been ringed, nephews."

"THE THREE RINGS OF YOUR SOUL, CHILDREN; YOU ARE OF US! GO WITH OUR BLESSING, SONS OF THE HOUSE OF PETRON. IN YOUR MANNER, DO WHAT YOU NEED TO DO."

The figures faded from sight, but Mikal and Ralton knew they would be there in his heart. They now understood what the ancestri were; they were the souls of their people and they could be with them if they so chose. Mikal looked at his uncle, and then at Ralton.

"I guess you know we're going to Abor." Mikal said. Then he smiled as he looked again at Gherrict. "I'm speaking Aborian, aren't I?"

"You speak it nicely." Gherrict told him. "Is what you

experienced still shit?"

"No, it isn't." Mikal said. Both men and boy were covered in sweat

Mikal's face grew somber. "I can't go without explaining this to one other person at the least."

"Who?" Asked his uncle

"My sister, Jennifer."

CHAPTER FOUR

EXPLANATIONS AND LEAVINGS

There was further training another week and a half. During that time, he was cut off from the one person he loved as much as his son. His sister, Jennifer Tanya Hamilton, the first born of his mother's marriage to Max Hamilton.

Michael hated him. "Son of a bitch" was the nicest thing he could say about the man. There were two other siblings, Joe Morgan and Stephanie Shania Hamilton. Mikal liked them well enough but he wasn't close to them. Somehow, they seemed to take the side of the kids who mocked him for his looks. He heard from his stepfather who kept calling him every name he could think of. After all, Michael wasn't his. When he was drunk, the others never had to fear their father. He took it out on his wife's bastard. Amazingly enough, Max didn't do anything front of Sandra at first. It was when the drinking got worse that he began to strike Michael. The drinking got bad enough even Sandra got hit if she got between the two. Sandra finally divorced Max. He retained visitation with the children. Michael left the house when Max came over.

School was worse. There were more than a few youngsters that accused Michael of wearing contact lenses because of his blue-green eyes. He was in many fights because of them and the ears that came to a definite point. He was, still for most people, black. They didn't like what they thought was fakery on his part. Michael learned to fight. This had the net effect of making sure the teasing came from a safe distance. It left him feeling outside of most things that went on at school. It also left him a lot of time to dream and work toward his dreams. Let them laugh he thought. It simply meant he had more time to do the things he really wanted to do. He bought a super eight millimeter camera and started to experiment with film. He later got a used video camera and experimented with that. He combined acting with film effects cut into the video. He'd seen those sort of effects on several series from England. He thought it was a good idea.

Michael did make friends in school. They were seemingly as outside of everything as he was. One was Donald "Duck" Raines. He wanted to be a cameraman when he grew up. Making movies with Michael allowed both boys to experiment making their productions. They pooled their money and shared the equipment they bought. Both worked on the films making the props and doing what they could for special effects. Michael did what he could for music by composing it to the best of his ability. Both made sure they got copies of the result and they were brutal with their own criticism. They knew they would make it in their desired professions. This continued as they grew up and matured. They would not let their dreams die no matter what people said about them or their attempts at film making.

Michael pushed himself harder in school. He knew he would need it as he grew up. Learning to fight, he defended himself and his half-siblings when he found them being teased and made miserable for their relationship with him. Joe and Stephanie withdrew from him and joined in the teasing. Jennifer stopped when she saw the pain it caused him or caught the tears of frustration he tried to hide. It was tough enough on him. That his younger brother and sister would join in made it harder. Eventually, he learned to stifle the tears and swallow the pride. Joe and Stephanie found they lost a defender when Michael turned his back on them.

Jennifer Hamilton, the eldest of his mother's marriage to his stepfather Max Hamilton, was different. That relationship grew as Michael improved his music playing. He taught Jennifer what he learned. Eventually, they would duet on the pieces they learned. Jennifer even began to play keyboards at church for the junior choir.

Max on the other hand, didn't care for the music, the movie making or the growing friendship between brother and sister. Max smashed several guitars Michael owned. Michael would work harder to replace them. That did not sit well with Max; "You damned fucking freak!" spat out of him on more than one occasion. When he caught Michael alone, he beat him if he could catch him. Sandra did her best to protect her son until she realized she couldn't have this man in her life. It was too important to her to keep the children alive; she was supporting her family by herself anyway. She filed for divorce. Sandra Stone also got a restraining order against Max.

One night he came to the house screaming for Sandra to come out of the house. When she didn't, he forced his way in. The terrified woman got Joe, Stephanie and Jennifer out of the house and over to a neighbor's house. Michael stayed behind clutching a baseball bat; he hid in the house making sure Max didn't see him.

He crept out of his hiding place and saw his ex-stepfather holding Sandra down. He'd beaten her and was about to rape her.

Max didn't see the baseball bat coming for his head. Michael got two blows to Max's head and started on his ribs and continued to hit his head until Max rolled off of Sandra. Michael got several blows to Max's crotch making the man curl up in a fetal position. That didn't stop Michael from raining blows on Max and making the man scream out. The thirteen-year-old boy didn't stop until the police came into the room and pulled him off of Max. The neighbors had called the police when they heard the sound of the brutal beating coming from the house. The bat was covered with blood and hate burned in Michael's eyes.

As the police pulled Max out of the house, he looked back at his ex-stepson. Michael's eyes told the story. If he came back to the house ever again, he would die. The eyes said everything the boy would not. Sandra held her brave son who did not let go of the baseball bat. Michael's eyes followed the car as it pulled away with Max in it. Once inside, Michael finally broke down and cried in his mother's arms.

Max was a broken man and he knew enough he had to stay away. The next time he saw his ex-wife, it was in divorce court. His nose was broken. Michael would not stop staring at him with hate filled eyes. Once the divorce was granted, Max walked out of their lives for good.

Sandra Stone was a pretty black woman who worked for the local telephone company. Thail Marius Petron told her he was a foreign exchange student when the two met. They made an odd couple. He was fair and charming and she was a smoldering woman with a honey complexion and black hair. It wasn't love at first. The fascination grew until the obvious wasn't important. He wined her and dined her and finally charmed her. She showed him around the town and helped him understand her people. Thail liked learning about different people. They took in ball games of every kind. Thail especially loved basketball, even learning the game well enough so he could play in pickup games. There were the occasional concerts; picnics, boat trips and drives up the coast in the nineteen sixty-eight Mustang Thail bought. He truly liked this brown skinned woman with the heart shaped face and full sensual lips and a body that demanded love.

They became friends then lovers. Two years passed. They decided to celebrate by going out on a boat. Their friends invited them to go out and be a foursome. Thail drove himself and Sandra out to the marina. Their friends would be there before them. Even a cloudy, overcast day couldn't dampen their spirits.

Dave's boat was a beautiful thirty-foot cabin cruiser. They left enjoying the ride and laughing with each other. It was perfect despite everything.

The weather changed and the water got choppy. "You know, if it gets choppier, I'll take her in." Dave said. He didn't like ignoring the feeling in his stomach. As a swell hit the boat and pushed the prow up and then dropped it the water. "I hope that's the last of that!"

They sat there for a few seconds and things seemed to calm. They looked at each other and laughed.

"I guess that's just nature's way of letting you know who is boss!" Thail cracked. He got up on the prow of the boat. "I'm king of the world!" he shouted and threw his arms out in victory. The boat rose up again and dropped down, hard in the water. Thail lost his footing and fell in the water. He struggled to get back to the boat. There was something in the water with him. He kicked at it and pulled away as the others in the boat shouted at him to make for the life preserver. Although his life jacket was doing its job, he felt something grab him and pull him down. His hands were pinned to his back and he could feel restraints locking his wrists together, then his feet. An air mask was slipped on his face.

On the boat the others saw Thail go under. Somehow, all knew he wasn't coming up. Why didn't they see blood?

"Sandy, I think the current got him!" Whitney said. "I don't think he's coming up!"

Sandra held her stomach. Did they just lose the baby's father? Sandra went to the front of the boat.

"Sandra, he isn't coming up," Dave said. "I think he's gone."

"Dear Lord, no." Sandra said. She started to scream Thail's name over and over. The weather changed again, the skies got darker and the water rougher.

"Sandy, I'm sorry. We have to go back in. There isn't anything we can do." Dave said. Whitney had to pry Sandra's fingers from the railing and get her back to a seat. Dave took the boat back to the marina.

Thail found himself being dragged to a submersible like none other on Earth. He was put into the waiting hatch and loaded in like so much meat. Once he was aboard and his hands freed, he furiously ripped the air mask off. He stared into the white haired man's eye and said "Damn you! At least you could have let me see if it were a boy or a girl!"

The man standing in front of him smiled. "Brother, I am not interested in your affairs with your trollops."

Thail got in his face. "Sandra is no trollop!" He accepted

the towel and began to wipe his hair down. "At the very least, let me provide something for her."

"That has been done, Thail. She will receive the benefits of your insurance policy."

"Insurance policy?" Thail asked.

"She will receive two million American dollars. We are generous."

"If not a little inconvenient." Thail said.

Gherrict sighed. "Thail, Thail, Thail. Our father wants his chosen heir with him, not attending to a pregnant mistress on another world. Now clean yourself up. You look like a drowned rat. It will not do having you look like that that when you meet your mother here."

"Mother's here?!" Thail's jaw dropped.

"She is aboard the mother ship. You don't think she'd actually come down here, do you?" Gherrict smiled.

"You bastard," Thail said with disgust.

"Like so many of your children, my brother." Gherrict said.

Thail wore a sour look. "Make sure Sandra gets the money before the child comes. I'm going to change." He stalked off as Gherrict smirked at his retreating back.

"I'll be blessed; he really does care about her." Gherrict said.

"Michael John Stone, that's his name." Sandra said to Whitney, Dave and her sister Bertha as they looked on the mother and child. Michael had Thail's ears and the oddity of his parentage gave him bright blue-green eyes.

"He is adorable!" Whitney said as she cooed at the baby.

"He is a champ!" Dave agreed as he tickled the newborn under the chin.

The baby yawned and went to sleep in his mother's arms. Sandra took the baby over to the bassinet and lay him down and tucked him in.

"Sandy, we've got to go." Whitney said as she gathered her coat.

Dave pulled on his overcoat and kissed Sandra on the cheek. "We'll see you later, okay? Get some rest. You've been through a lot."

Sandra watched as the two left. Bertha wore a frown. Sandra saw it and sighed. "Okay, say it."

"Maybe you were lucky to lose that Thail. I mean for all you know, he could have been there for a quick hit and run."

"After two years?" asked Sandra. "The man was there for the long haul, old woman."

"I hate it when you call me old woman."

"Then stop acting like one." Sandra said. "You work too hard at being a bitch, do you know it? You forget, he made me the beneficiary of his insurance policy. How many men do you know would do that with a cool two million dollars?"

"That don't mean nothing." Bertha said coldly. "You had no business running around with that white man."

"Oh, now it comes out. He's white." Sandra said. "He

treated me better than ninety percent of the men either one of us knew. You can't handle that, can you?"

"At least I didn't get pregnant by no white boy who got killed because he couldn't stay off the front of the boat!" Bertha said.

"You're just jealous! That's all that is!" Sandra declared. "Thail loved me! At least I didn't get fucked over by all the men I ever dated!" Sandra took a breath. "Don't take your jealousy out on me! If you can't handle it, get the hell out!" She pointed at the door. "Don't let the door hit you on the way out!"

Bertha Stone got up out of her chair and went to the door. She stopped and turned to her younger sister. "You have been through a great deal today with the birth of your child. I am going to be a good Christian woman and leave you in peace. I know I am right and I am going to pray for you. I think that man was the devil himself and you just had his baby."

Sandra sat there stupefied. She then picked up a vase of flowers off the stand near her bed and threw it at her sister's head. Bertha ducked out the door quickly and closed it behind her.

"One of us is wrong and I know it isn't me." Sandra said to the door. She knew she would tell her son about his father as soon as the boy was old enough to ask. He would also know how much his father loved them both.

Sandra took the two million dollars and made the best

life she could for them. For about two years more she juggled her baby and her studies and finally became the lawyer she wanted to be. Sandra also made sure that there was money put away for Michael's education. She wanted to make sure he didn't have to struggle like she did in school.

However, a year after she had her son, Sandra and Bertha were on better speaking terms. Bertha even introduced Sandra and Max to each other. She thought they were a cute couple. Bertha was no good judge of character.

Max gave no sign of his true character until after they were married. Then it was a slap, and then an apology. A punch and then I'm sorry. He could quit for a while to let her forget. But for Michael, there were no apologies nor would there ever be.

This went on and off for twelve years.

The phone on the other end started to ring bringing Michael back to the present.

"Hello?" it was Bertha.

"This Michael. Is Jenny in?"

"Now what makes you think she wants to talk to you?" Bertha's voice was ice. "I don't think she needs to talk to you."

Michael counted to ten, and then spoke. "Bertha, do you remember the time I had to come over to talk to Jenny because you wouldn't call her to the phone? How is Donnell anyway?" Donnell was Bertha's oldest son, a six foot two hundred pound man who worked out. The fight put him in the hospital, and Donnell hadn't been able to walk properly since.

There was a long silence. "I'll put her on."

"Thank you." Michael said. He heard the phone placed on a table and then it was picked up.

"Hello?"

"Hi, baby sis." Michael said.

"Mike, where have you been?" Jennifer asked. He could hear the upset and concern in her voice. "I have been calling your place and keep getting a voice telling me that you and Ralt were 'out for the day' for three weeks! What is going on? Are you in trouble? I have been afraid to come over there!"

Michael took a deep breath. "Jen, you know Bertha's listening on the other phone and this is none of her business. Come on over?"

"I'm on my way over!"

"Thank you, sis, see you when you get here."

"Bye."

"Bye."

They hung up at the same time. Jennifer got a light sweater and her bag, checked for her car keys and made for the door she found Bertha blocking.

"Bertha, I got to go, would you please move?" Jennifer said.

"I heard what he said." Bertha spat. "You don't owe that boy nothing!"

"I don't know what your problem is with Mike."

Jennifer said. "He hasn't done anything to you. You gave him hell when he lived with us. Hell, you forced him to take the baby and live in that van of his!" Her arms went akimbo. "Now, I don't know why you don't like him, and I don't care. That is my brother over there. He has helped take care of me, Joe, and Stephanie ever since mama died and I am not about to start letting him down now."

"I am telling you that boy is spawn of the devil and you refuse to believe me! I've shown you the pictures!" Bertha said.

"You kept those pictures from him! Those pictures belong to him!" Jennifer said. "Then, you went and hid them so I couldn't find them and show them to him! You really work at being a bitch, don't you?! Besides, you shouldn't have been listening in any way!"

"I pay the bills on that phone. I will listen in if I want to." Bertha declared.

"That is my brother over there. Take that ass out of my way!" Jennifer told her as she push past her infuriated aunt.

Bertha watched as Jennifer drove off. "Grab your ass and take it out of the way!" She slammed the door closed.

In front of Michael's apartment, Jennifer parked her Escort and then got out of the car. As she locked it, she looked up stairs at the window of the apartment. She wondered what was going on in there. Once she was on the fourth floor, she noticed two huge, well-muscled men in black with dark copper-colored glasses standing to either side of the door. She took a deep breath and walked up to the apartment. As she approached the door, one of the men opened it saying; "please go in, Miss Hamilton."

Jennifer swallowed her questions and entered. A smiling man approached her. "Good morning, Miss Hamilton, May I take your sweater and bag? You won't need it." Jennifer handed them over. "My name is Valegen."

"You're like Michael's daddy. She knew because she'd seen the pictures her mother had." Jennifer said. Suddenly, it hit her. They were why she couldn't reach her brother and nephew. All the questions seem to filter down to what Michael would tell her.

"Yes, we are. However, My Lord Mikal would like to be the one to explain." He led her to the closet. "Please go in."

"This is the closet." Jennifer said. "Michael is not royalty."

"As I said, he would like to explain." Valegen smiled indulgently. "Please, go in."

Jennifer stepped slowly into the closet. Her jaw dropped as she felt a slight breeze. She went back to the closet door and looked back into the room she was so familiar with; she turned back into the strange room and stared; something was too strange, too weird and it was happening now.

Jennifer made her way back into the "room" staring dumbfounded at the sight of an open sky, clear blue and fresh smelling. The breezes played gently against her skin and leaves scampered across the ground. They seemed to be in some kind of valley with a flowing stream, beautiful flowers and lush grass. There was a gazebo a few hundred yards from the door and she saw two figures sitting at the table in it. There was some kind of servant pouring something into a glass. As she drew closer, she could see Michael, Ralton and a...a..no it was too crazy, a butler.

"Thank you, Arvis." Michael said as he picked up the cup of green tea and sipped. He looked around and spotted Jennifer staring with disbelief at the sights and sounds around her.

The butler pulled the chair out for her. "For my lady." The butler said.

Jennifer sat down and stared at her brother and nephew as they settled in their chairs. "What is going on here Mike?"

Ralt giggled as if he still couldn't believe it. Michael smiled at her and his son. "You want the long version or the short version?"

"Yeah." Was all she could say.

Michael smiled and began. More than once Jennifer interrupted him to clarify something. Ralt chimed in with information when his father took a drink from his water glass. Jennifer told them they were both crazy.

"How the hell could your father be on this planet without anyone knowing it?" Jennifer asked.

"How many undocumented aliens from other countries are here?" asked Michael. "You know that people come into this country every day by any means necessary. He was here apparently just looking around and found mom. They met, fell in love and I was the result."

Jennifer sat back in disbelief. "Now he wants you? That man doesn't know you!"

"I know that. However, he hasn't given me much of a choice; so, I'm going forward." Michael said. "Look, why don't we take a walk? I'll feel a little better about what I have to say."

"Sure." Jennifer said.

They got up and walked for some time. Michael told her about everything except the ancestri. It wasn't that he didn't think she could handle it, he just felt there was enough to explain with his and Ralt's leaving. His voice was heavy with exhaustion and the environment's swirling colors were relaxing. There was sweet music playing. It sounded something like Bach meets Ellington played on alien wind instruments and a glass harp and subtle tubular bells.

Valegen approached them. "Brunch is served My lord. If you will follow me?"

"Lead on McValegen." Michael said. "Anyway, that's that. Now you know what I know."

"If I were you, I would be running like Flo-Jo." Jennifer said. "I cannot believe you're an alien prince." She looked him over. "You still look like my older brother."

"I always will be." Michael put an arm around her. "Just like you will be my baby sis. I have to go. When I accepted the shopping spree, I accepted the deal."

"Sounds like a raw deal." Jennifer told him.

"I want to meet this father of mine and thank him very much for everything he's done so far." They arrived at the table and sat down. Ralt was eating as they sat down and he knew enough not to ask. He knew what the conversation was about anyway.

"Look, I know they are wrong in the way they did it," Jennifer said firmly, "But you will be on their world and who knows how they will react if you do anything stupid."

"I'm not gonna do anything stupid!" Michael protested.

Jennifer fixed him with a "who are you talking to" look. "You know you will. You better hope they don't decide to take you out like yesterday's garbage."

Michael knew enough not to argue when his sister knew him so well. "Fine, I'll play it cool and see what I'm finally dealt."

"That's better." Jennifer said as she looked over the spread. "Have you been eating like this since they told you?"

"It starts at breakfast, and then we suffer all day." Michael said. "The pain is just too much."

Jennifer hit him with her napkin. "You a fool!" Michael laughed as he dug into his food.

CHAPTER FIVE

A CONVERSATION BEFORE LIFTOFF

The next day, Jennifer found herself invited to lunch. It wouldn't have bothered her except the invitation came from one of the uncles Michael introduced her to. She could see the relationship and she wondered what they wanted to speak to her for. After all, they had what they wanted, they didn't need to see her. The questions ate at her as she drove to the restaurant.

The day before, Urgess, Valegen and Gherrict watched from another 'room' as the family ate together. As the lunch ended they listened as Michael said, "I raised hell to get you, Joe and Stephanie money to do what you want to do. It isn't unlimited and you'll have to be careful, but you should be okay. I just wish there was some way to keep in contact with you, tell you what's happening with us." He looked at her sadly. "I don't want to lose any of you, not even Joe or Stephanie. He gave a little nervous laugh. "We've been through too much to lose each other," Suddenly, his expression changed, he held her close and soaked her shoulder with tears.

"My Lords, blood is blood even here. Can we afford to try and break these obviously deep bonds completely?" Valegen asked.

Urgess rubbed his temples slowly. "No, we cannot."

"We should give something to her," Gherrict added, "I have never seen such love and devotion in my life. Their kin bond is deep and should not be destroyed."

"I agree, brother, that relationship is part of his strength. It must be preserved." Urgess spoke. "I think lunch is a good idea." He looked at his aide. "Please arrange it, Valegen."

Valegen smiled. "It is my pleasure, my Lords." He left.

"You should really talk to him, Urgess." Gherrict said as he watched him leave.

Urgess looked at Gherrict. "Why?"

"He engineers too many attempts at happy endings." Gherrict replied.

"Hypocrite," Urgess said, "you want to talk to this girl as much as I do. You are intrigued by her as I am."

"I suppose you think this is the right thing to do?" asked Gherrict sardonically.

"A small going away present wouldn't be amiss." Urgess said.

Gherrict nodded. "Good idea."

"I do have them." Urgess defended.

"It is nice to know miracles happen." Gherrict told him. Urgess shot him a dirty look.

She pulled into the lot, parked and went in all the while trying not to act like a tourist. It was a quiet place with private booths. Jennifer showed up dressed in her best serious clothes when she heard where they would be. The Standard was a four star restaurant with a reputation for excellence. It may not matter to others but Jennifer made sure she was as much as possible, all that.

She spotted Valegen standing near a door. It had to be one of the fabled private booths. Damn, she thought, he looks like he belongs here. How was it possible to stand so openly waiting for someone and manage to be inconspicuous?

"Good afternoon, Miss Jennifer, they're waiting for you." Valegen opened the door. She entered and he followed and closed the door. He pulled out a chair for her. He sat at a small table.

Jennifer looked over the two men before her. The one with the silver-white hair had to be Gherrict. She understood why the man unnerved her brother. He threw off a palatable aura of power with no wasted energy, sitting like a crouching tiger, waiting to strike.

The other had to be Urgess. He was urbane, smooth and dark haired. He was relaxed, but Jennifer knew that could be a pretext. If Gherrict was ready to strike, Urgess seemed to know what he would do when he needed to do it. If Jennifer knew about the ancestri and the power it granted, she would have done her best to keep her nerves calm. As it was her ignorance was a good thing.

Urgess started it off. "It seems we owe you an explanation, Miss Hamilton."

"I'd say you do." Jennifer said. "First you trash my brother's name. You see to it that unless he had a phalanx of lawyers he couldn't undo the damage done to him. You couldn't be men and tell him who you were and why you were here so he could make up his own mind?" She humped. "I know you owe me a good reason why I don't call the police."

Gherrict spoke up. "Most likely, you would not be believed, and you would be dismissed without the evidence to prove what you were saying was true. Believe me, Miss Hamilton we knew what we were doing."

"Yeah, and you did it all over Michael." Jennifer shot back. "You are so lucky he regards this as an adventure he's been waiting for all his life."

Urgess smiled. "Yes, you are quite right. He does regard this as an adventure. The fact is we need Mikal Jon. Ralton Jon is definitely a bonus."

"That is my family you're taking. If anything happens to them, I will make you wish you weren't born." Jennifer said. "That may sound crazy, but I will go Old Testament on your asses."

"Old Testament?" puzzled Urgess.

"It is the first half of the Christian Bible." Gherrict said. "Trust me it is not a pretty statement she just made." He looked at Jennifer. "I believe she would do it, too."

"Damn straight." Jennifer said. "Why do you need him anyway?"

"We have made mistakes with some of our children and we believe your brother will be the one to help correct them." Urgess told her.

"That is completely stupid! You're the ones who made the mess!" Jennifer stated. "Mike told me what you told him. He wouldn't say why or how he is to do it. That doesn't make any sense."

"He is to be the seed for change. We need him, please believe that. We can't tell you more than that. We have said too much already." Urgess said.

"You're very much like your mother." Gherrict said. "When I came to get Mikal's father, I observed her. She was a courageous woman, very pretty. I understood why Mikal's father fell for her. He also said she could be the most level headed person in the room in times of crisis."

"You saw my mother?" asked Jennifer.

"Yes. She and Mikal's father made a handsome couple." Gherrict told her. "But we had need of him at home. It was time for him to take the throne and rule our world. He was not happy when he had to leave. To help her we left two million of your dollars for her and the baby. We still kept a watch over him. We also saw you and your other siblings grow up as well."

Jennifer sat back with her mouth open. She didn't want to believe it. Unbidden, her mind flew back to the times out of the corner of her eye when she would catch sight of someone watching her and her family, ducking just out of sight when they were spotted. She remembered the times when Michael would find part time work when no one else had any. The employer, now that she thought about it, looked a lot like these two men. The memories came faster; kindly old Doctor Riley who hired him to do his lawn every week. Mr. Shelly, a musician who encouraged him and gave him some music lesson for chores done around the big two story place he owned. Miss Yvonne who tutored and encouraged him when he needed academic help.

"All those times I thought Michael was simply lucky to meet people who helped him," Jennifer said, "there were all these people I remember seeing, and, they would just move so I wouldn't really see them. They were your people!" She put her hand to her mouth and then dropped it. "All those times he found jobs to earn a little money. His account never went dry after he paid Jessie off! That was all of you watching him. Damn!" She looked at all of them in shock. "That's why he stopped having real money troubles and found what he needed at the last moment. You kept his account open."

"It was a simple matter to make sure he was solvent." Gherrict said. "Since he was always a thrifty one, it wasn't difficult. All we really had to do was make sure that he got the money after the sub sector government gave him his pittance for the month. I'm quite sure he never told anyone."

"He sure didn't tell me!" Jennifer said.

"It was understandable since his benefits would be reduced if he did reveal what was happening to anyone." Urgess added. "Mikal was smarter than anyone would have thought."

Jennifer sat silently for a while. It took her a little while to process this. She would bet money that Michael had no idea what was happening. It would make sense for him not to tell anyone since it might get back to the authorities. She knew the time he spent in Bertha's house was some of the worst times he ever had. Jennifer knew her brother was a survivor. Now these three strangers were telling her they helped him to survive the difficult time by making sure he never hurt over what he didn't have. "I suppose you want me to keep quiet about this?"

"If you would," Gherrict said. "It is more important that Mikal not know. I'm sure he will find out on his own."

Jennifer shook her head. "Y'all crazy. I'll keep my mouth shut but he will find out eventually." She took a drink from her water glass. "You weren't going to let him go down, were you?"

"We take care of our own in this family. Mikal is family." Urgess said.

Jennifer nodded. "Why do you call him 'Mikal'?"

"That is how we will be saying his name on our home world." Urgess explained. "Look, I know this doesn't look good."

"Who are you telling?!" Jennifer interrupted.

The three men looked at each other; Valegen simply gave a small shrug. He wasn't the one in trouble. Urgess and Gherrict knew the young woman in front of them was angry with them for this disruption of their lives. The destruction of her brother's name was more than she could stand. Now they were taking him and his son to their world. Jennifer hated the feeling of helplessness. She looked at them, these aliens and wondered if they knew what they have done. It almost didn't matter, her anger; it didn't matter how much she would miss this brother and how much he would miss her. Jennifer opened her bag and pulled out a tissue and dabbed at the tears that started at the corners of her eyes.

"Shit." she said softly.

For once in his life words failed Urgess. Gherrict simply kept his silence. Valegen could feel the moment growing awkward. He reached under his table and pulled out what looked like a large sample case.

"This is a pulsar communicator. You can record voice messages and send them to Abor. It is set to send to a small satellite we have placed in orbit to boost the signal and send it to us. It's lucky for us that your people don't have one of your shuttles in space this week."

"I was wondering about that. How do you keep us from seeing your ship?" asked Jennifer.

Urgess smiled. "We're parked on the other side of your moon. Even with your space telescope up there, you still can't see through a star body. Believe me when I say it isn't easy to plan these things."

"I'll bet." Jennifer replied. She turned the case around and looked at the controls. They were clearly labeled and she tried them to get a feel for them. They were simple enough and she felt confident after a few moments. "This thing is real simple."

"Yes it is," Gherrict said, "we give them to our explorers when they go to other worlds and they have an emergency. It's very powerful."

"What about this satellite?" Jennifer asked. "Somebody's going to find it."

"It is well hidden among the ones in orbit. They will not know what is out there since there is so much up there already." Urgess said. "That is an advantage of a planet just getting into space, they put so much up and they don't take down what is obsolete since it would cost too much. Trust me. they will not know it is there."

Jennifer had to take them at their word. "You know, Michael's written about this sort of thing. He's even written down ideas about how the stuff would work. Every time I read one of his stories, I always felt like it could happen. Now it is," she shook her head. "Michael never told anyone about the pictures he found with his dad in them. Our aunt thought she hid them from him; he had copies made and then put them back where she had them. He put his copies in his van; she never went near it." She looked at them. "Michael always knew he was different; he just didn't know how different."

She closed the case and sat it down next to her chair.

"We shouldn't tear you apart." Urgess said. "That was never part of our mandate from Michael's father."

"It ain't part of mine either." Jennifer told him. "It may sound stupid. If anything happens to him, we will have to dance."

"I do believe I know the steps already." Gherrict said. He looked at his companions. "Shall we order lunch?"

It was a week later when Jennifer found herself, Michael and Ralton standing at a small airstrip in what looked like the middle of nowhere. The land was newly deeded to one Jennifer Hamilton and she was amazed that she owned it. She looked around when she drove up in her new Mercedes. That was a gift along with a quarter million dollars to her. The money was Michael's doing. He didn't want to leave her with nothing. Joe and Stephanie would get the same if they stayed in school and off drugs. Michael had a bet with Jennifer their siblings couldn't do it.

Ralton held onto his aunt fiercely and it took some effort to pull him off. The brother and sister held each other and whispered their goodbyes.

"Please my lord. We must leave before we are detected by the local authorities. Their equipment might be primitive, but it works well enough to notice something." Valegen said.

Michael and Jennifer let go of each other and she got into her car and drove a mile away from the area. It wouldn't do to have her there when the ship lifted off. It wasn't very big, about the size of a 707 jet. It had VTOL and the pilot engaged the system and got the ship off the ground with a minimum of noise. It would circle the world and then slingshot out of the atmosphere. If they did it right, they would leave with a minimum of fuss.

Jennifer watched the ship leave through binoculars. She thought about the adventure her brother was embarking on, smiling, knowing everything Michael dreamed was about to happen. "Good luck, baby." She got back into her car and drove home to her own future.

Aboard the ship, Michael and Ralton watched a screen showing them the planet as they left. Michael wished they hadn't watched. He didn't want the feelings he was fighting to leave him a blubbering mess as they left his home. They broke atmosphere and saw the planet drop away from them.

"Wow." was all Ralton could say.

"Yeah." Michael said. "'bye, you big blue marble."

The mother ship was parked on the other side of the moon. The newly aware king's son was about to land and they would leave as soon as he came aboard.

As their shuttle rounded the moon, they became aware how big the ship was. To Michael's estimation, it was as big as three L.A. Coliseums laid end to end. "Whoa!" Michael said as the ship came closer.

"Dang, that thing is big!" Ralton said.

"I hope it has a hospital." muttered Michael, the anger coming back into his voice.

Valegen heard him and saw the anger was now resurfacing. "My lord, I urge caution. You could be putting your son in danger."

"And he hasn't done that already?" sneered Michael. "He ruins my name and takes my choices away from me! He has already put my son in danger!"

Gherrict glared at him, thinking the anger was settled in Mikal. He was aware of how little that glare mattered to Michael right now.

Urgess said "Mikal, if it makes you feel any better, we were the ones who laid out the final plans, take your anger out on us. Please!" He looked desperately at Gherrict, and then turned back to Michael, "Let him explain why this happened!" He wiped his face. "Gods, we've told you why!"

Gherrict said, "what can it cost you to listen?"

"You mean, besides what it cost me already?" spat Michael.

Valegen spoke up "My lord, these are your people, they are waiting for you. Please, don't do anything foolish."

"Val, you're a nice dude, but guess what? They are only here to see what freaks you brought from the planet." Michael said.

Gherrict's eyes narrowed. "Jon, do not be obstinate. What has happened, has happened. Whatever you plan on doing will not change it."

Mikal gave the three a cold smile. Ralt sank into his chair knowing his father wore his steel toed boots. Gherrict took the studded gloves, but forgot to check the footwear.

The ship entered the berth safely coming to a complete stop; as it did, the passengers removed the face masks and disembarked. Gherrict and Urgess got off first with Mikal, Ralton and Valegen following. An elaborately dressed couple slowly approached the two uncles. The king was tall, white haired and ruggedly handsome. Michael could see where he got his looks from. Ralt was startled to see how much his father looked like his grandfather. The king wore elaborate embroidered clothes with a short ornate cape. Ralt thought that he and his father were under dressed. There was an air about him of being completely in control. He knew who he was and that he was the master of his world. The queen was beautiful with a heart shaped face and deep red hair. Her smile glowed and she had an air of serenity and calm. Just like mom, Michael thought. This was going to hurt.

Valegen held Michael by the elbow with a strong grip. Valegen knew this was not enough to stop Michael from doing whatever he wanted. He simply hoped it would remind him not to do anything foolish.

"He looks better than he did in the photographs!" Ralton said quietly.

"Yeah, I guess," was all Michael could say. He could feel the fury at this man, this elder doppelganger, building inside. They didn't have to ruin his name to get him here, but the man didn't even know that part. Michael stopped at Valegen's instruction. They stayed back a few feet while Urgess and Gherrict spoke with the king.

For the occasion, Mikal wore a dark blue tunic with an open collar with black slacks and Doc Martin boots. Ralt wore the same except that he wore the boots Gherrict gave him.

Father and son stopped short of the royal couple. Valegen stepped behind Ralt. Urgess stepped to the king's right, Gherrict to the queen's left. Urgess gave Michael a warning with his eyes. "Your Majesties," Urgess said gesturing toward Michael and Ralt, "may I introduce to you Mikal Jon Ston-Petron of Earth and his son Ralton Jon Ston-Petron. Ralton is eleven standard years of age." He looked nervously at Mikal. "Mikal Jon, these are their majesties. Your King and father, Thail Marius Petron, and his Queen and wife Uasar Asue Petron of the planet Aboria."

Mikal sucker punched Thail, breaking the king's jaw. The king attempted to get up only to receive a kick to the ribs, breaking some. Gherrict and Urgess rushed and held him back. That was all he was going to get as they pinned his arms behind him. Valegen took Ralt away and closed his eyes sadly. He knew something like this was going to happen.

The queen stared at Mikal. "Why? Why do this?"

"He wasn't man enough to come talk to me himself! He sends these two." Mikal tilted his head toward Gherrict, "to come ruin my name and make it so I had no choice about coming on this trip. He endangers my son, and trashed my reputation... FOR WHAT!? I had a life, damn it, and he had no right to do me like that!" Gherrict and Urgess dragged Mikal off as attendants picked up the dazed king and took him to the sick bay. "What did you do to deserve him?!"

Uasar stared at the retreating forms and looked over at Ralton who was shaking in Valegen's hands. She then looked up and saw the many half-breed crew members smiling and discussing what just happened from their catwalk. It was only the royals on the floor as she and her husband greeted Mikal. The half-breeds weren't allowed on the same level with the royals and the queen knew they regarded Mikal as just one more lab animal to be sacrificed.

Uasar looked at Ralton. What his father just did scared him as well. She knew the boy had no idea what would happen next. "Please see to it that Ralton gets settled in Valegen."

"Of course, my queen." Valegen said. "Come along, Ralton, I will show you to your rooms." He led Ralton away.

The queen was lost in thought as she saw the approval and glee the ship's half-breeds wore. They've just been reawakened, she thought. She knew they had cameras and many taped the arrival. There was no way to keep this from getting out. Aborian media already had the story. The half-breeds were happy about what happened. For the full-bloods, Mikal would be controversial.

"Well, the pot's been stirred." The queen said softly to herself. She then went to sickbay.

CHAPTER SIX

A WALK AROUND

As Valegen led Ralton to his rooms on the ship, the boy's head swiveled every way to take in as much as he could. The ship was everything and beyond what he expected. Ralton stopped often to watch people at work just to see what they did.

From the ship's docking bay they went into a long hall lined with lush wood paneling and deep carpeting in a rich blue with the royal crest. Ralton liked the look of the uniforms and the people who wore them. Suddenly, they came into an opening and Ralt stopped and his jaw dropped. They were in a gathering place that was three levels deep. It looked like a theater. There was a spiral ramp leading to all three levels and they could see the ones above and below.

"Whoa!" Ralt said as he took it all in.

"Yes," Valegen said, "it is quite impressive, isn't it? This is where, if it isn't canceled, your welcoming dinner will be held."

"Are you sure? After dad dropped the king, I would think it would be off." said Ralt as he ran his hand along the smooth railing. "I wish he hadn't done that."

"As do I, young Ralton." Valegen sighed. "In many ways, it was a good thing."

Ralt looked Valegen. "What do you mean?"

"Your grandfather, like most Aborians, underestimates people like your father. Many people, the full blood, the ones of Aborian stock only, assume the half-breed, the children whose blood is mixed of this and other worlds, will say or do nothing about what we do to them. Your father showed His Majesty that is wrong." Valegen explained. "Mikal is a proud man. He worked very hard for what he had. We took it away. Unfortunately, we've done the same to so many for so long, we've forgotten what it is like to have someone say 'no' to us. Your father said 'no' to us." He broke into a smile. "That may be the best thing that has happened in a long time." He put his hand on Ralton's shoulder. "Let's go."

Once out of there, they took the most direct route to where the apartments were. "This place is hardened against attack and will withstand most troubles. Your room is a life cell in case something should happen to the ship." Valegen told him. "Here we are." He pressed a button on the door and it slid open. Again Ralton's mouth dropped open.

The place was plush, lush and beyond anything Ralton had seen before. If the corridors leading here were this nice, it was nothing compared to the room he now stood in. "Dang!

Is everything on this ship like this?"

"Not everything. After all, this is part of the royal quarters. Your every need has been seen to. Anything you want at your command." Valegen said.

Ralt sat down on a chair and sank in. "Chain me to the wall!" He looked around and jumped up and ran into the other rooms. All were as lush as and more so than the front room. Ralt dove into the bed and bounced on it. He spread his arms out and let the luxury overtake him. He sighed with a deep satisfaction and closed his eyes. Valegen smiled as the boy took in what he never before experienced.

"Valegen?" asked Ralt.

"Yes, young lord?"

"Do you think the king will do anything to my dad for hitting him?"

Valegen sat on the bed next to the boy. He looked down and then at him. "By all rights, he should. To attack a king is a crime. However, I think there will be an outside chance he will not."

"Why not?" asked Ralt.

"The king needs your father. He needs someone with the ability to think for himself." Valegen explained. "Mikal has been without Thail most of his life. I agree with your father that the king should have presented himself and allowed Mikal to make up his own mind. The fact is, even without our help, Mikal would have made it to the job we got him fired from. He's a fighter, your father, and he was not about to allow anyone, even a king to get away with what we did." He fixed Ralt with a hard stare. "Your road will be easier because of your father. By striking the king, he served notice there will be none of the nonsense that most half-breeds have put up with for so long." Ralt was staring at him. "Your father just proved he might be crazier than we are." He smiled and Ralt returned it knowing what Valegen meant.

"Yeah! I guess the king forgot who was my dad's other parent." Ralt said.

"Aye, he did. In any case, get rest, young lord. I will take you about the ship once you get settled." Valegen said.

Ralt sat up and removed his boots and Valegen took them over to a concealed closet opening it by passing his hand over a sensor and the door slid open. Valegen placed the boots on the floor and let the door close.

"Rest well, young lord." Valegen said as he went to the door and turned off the lights. He paused for a moment and watched Ralt crawl under the covers and fall asleep. He knew the boy was tired. It had been a long day. Valegen walked out the apartment and went to his own room. He wanted to sleep too but there was too much to do and he had to get to it.

In the corridor, a servant met him. "Hoy, Valegen! What do you think of the new one, eh?"

"I think it will be very interesting to have him, Marok." Valegen answered.

"After seeing the king go down, I know it will." Marok said gleefully.

"You approved of him striking the king?" asked Valegen.

"Well, yes and no." Marok hedged. "I won't deny it will make it harder for him. I also don't deny he sent a message to all the royals about being careful who you muck with. Even kings need to respect others' feelings and points of view."

"True but even Mikal Jon needs to respect the king." said Valegen. "After all, that was his father he struck."

"True again but his father struck first." Marok said. "I'm amazed the welcoming feast is still on."

"Yes. I think they should delay it and let them find their levels of comfort with each other. They need to talk first." Valegen said. "The feast will not be easy."

"If the king thinks it worth it, he'll do what he has to do." Marok said. "After all, he didn't raise the boy." He started off and then turned. "Mikal's not a boy, is he?" He gave a bow and left.

Valegen stopped and thought it over. "You're right; Mikal's not a boy." He turned in the direction of the apartment Ralt slept in and a smile crept over his face. "He's even done what you have not, my King. Ralton's the proof." He made his way to his quarters needing to talk to Urgess.

Mikal sat in the room his uncles put him in to cool off. Padded and locked from the outside it was meant to let him simmer down until he was ready to go out again. Mikal laughed. This was a hell of a room for "time outs". Still Mikal knew he was wrong and right for striking the king. He still would not apologize to the man since he felt he was the wronged one. Mikal knew Urgess and Gherrict were not coming for him for a while.

Gherrict wiped his hands on the heated towel and put it back into the unit that kept his towels warm. It would be sterilized for his next use. The bathroom, like much of the ship, was a display of opulence and Gherrict took no notice.

Gherrict sighed as he contemplated this nephew, Mikal. He knew the younger man was right in that Thail should have presented himself first. Gherrict knew from the stories Mikal wrote knew that he would have come with them in a moment's notice. Mikal was no fool. The moment he found out who had taken his life away, Mikal would have found some way to get even.

In any case, Gherrict and Urgess had their work cut out for them. There had to be some way to get Mikal and Thail to talk. There had to be words that had no anger in them; the rancor had to die down. Still, Mikal had what they needed and Gherrict was determined to see to it that he kept it. He looked into the lone room's mirror and saw himself in the younger man. Only the anticipation of seeing a new world had been dampened and the practical needs were paramount now. Gherrict stretched out his hand and summoned his jacket. He still had a lot of training with Mikal to do.

Urgess sat at his computer screen and watched Mikal in the cooling off room. Mikal lay down on the provided cot and closed his eyes. For a moment, Urgess thought he saw a resignation to his situation on his nephew's face. Urgess wondered if Mikal's sense of wonder gone. Was his ability to let the moment teach him gone as well? He hoped not; so much of what Mikal was, was in those things, the ability to dream, to see a future beyond what he had. Urgess knew Mikal and liked Mikal but he allowed for improvement in everything. Urgess wondered if Mikal still resented his father for what was done to him, or did those blows release the anger he felt? Thail, as king, had every right to punish Mikal in the worst possible way. Urgess knew that if Thail did punish Mikal for striking him, he could very well set everything back worse than it was.

That was the last thing anyone wanted or needed.

Thail lay on the hospital bed in an ill humor. Mikal struck him!

Thail could feel his blood boiling up in him. The anger was threatening to go out of control and the resentment of this bastard son of his was slowly taking over. Thail hated that Mikal resented what happened. Didn't his brothers explain why they needed him, why this happened the way it did?

He switched on the view from the padded room Mikal was in. Mikal was apparently sleeping no worse for the wear. Of course Mikal could sleep Thail thought. It wasn't his world, he didn't know me and what did he care if his father's world was about to explode if they couldn't find a solution to the half-breed problem? No matter how Thail could turn it over in his mind, there was no real problem for Mikal since it wasn't his world. If Thail dared to think about it he didn't show the respect for his son he wanted for himself. Thail did think about it and the air in his indignity escaped. Yes, Mikal struck him.

Yes as king he hated that.

Yes it was on his orders that Urgess and Gherrict brought him here.

And damn it all yes, he did destroy his son's name and reputation. Mikal could sleep and Thail couldn't. He was starting out on the wrong foot again and this time, the child in question didn't care his father was the ruler of a world. He cared he wasn't man enough to talk to his son.

Thail could feel everything in him fighting for control. The anger wanted front and center, but the feelings he had buried long ago were coming to the surface. He loved Mikal's mother and that was slowly but surely taking over. If he truly loved the woman, shouldn't he treat what they created with more consideration?

Out the corner of his eye, he could see Sandra standing with her arms crossed in that "you know what you should do" manner. Thail laughed as all the memories of his time with her came flooding back.

"Damn it, Sandra, bless you! You've given me a son that can do what I need." Thail said. He stopped because his ribs were still sore. The doctors were good but even they still needed time to allow for his healing.

Thail knew then he needed to set things right between

him and Mikal. It didn't matter how many reports he saw, he still didn't know this son. His brothers did and that gave them the advantage. Thail hit the intercom and summoned Gherrict and Urgess to him.

Mikal woke up from a very relaxing sleep. His head and eyes cleared and he remembered where he was. Oh, crap he thought. No matter how right he was, he never should have struck his father.

Damn, he thought, I can't really even call him that since I don't know him. He doesn't know me either, and that's part of what got him hurt.

Mikal was amazed he didn't feel the same resentment he felt when he first met him. He supposed the truth was, he really wanted to know this sire. He wanted to know who his father was and maybe that would explain so much about him. Practically, he needed to apologize for striking Thail if only to get both of them some room to maneuver. Mikal snorted in resigned humor. This wasn't the way he wanted to meet his father, and this wasn't the way to start off. That apology was looking better all the time.

Mikal sat up, stretched and then stood up and finished stretching. He yawned and was in the middle of it when the door opened. He saw a young boy at the door.

"My lord, it is time for the welcoming feast. You will need to get ready." The boy said.

"Oh, yeah, right." Mikal said. "What's your name?"

"Tanlon, sir." The boy replied.

"Well, Tanlon, if you could show me where I'm suppose to go, I'll get ready." Mikal said.

"That is my job sir." Tanlon smiled. "I am to be your call boy."

Mikal tried not to laugh. "We have got find a better name for your job." He followed Tanlon out.

Once in the apartment, Mikal could tell Ralt was gone. Where could that boy be? He thought.

"Lord Ralton is playing video games. He is dressed now, and Lord Gherrict thought it a good way to keep him clean."

"He doesn't know my son very well, does he?" Mikal said as he took the tunic off. "That boy could find a way to get dirty even in a vacuum." Mikal sat on the bed and removed his boots. Tanlon took them and put them into the closet. He opened the door wider and Mikal saw the suits of clothes.

"As you can see, my Lord, we have your size." Tanlon said. "It is all coordinated and all you need to do is pick one."

"No kidding!" Mikal was astonished. He got up and felt one of the suits. The fabric was fabulous to the touch, soft and silky. "I'm gonna feel like a fraud wearing these."

Tanlon didn't understand. "You are the king's son."

"Tanlon," Mikal began, "I've never had any of this. I've never worn clothes like this. It's kind of hard to wear it if you haven't earned it."

"Perhaps you will earn it." Tanlon said. "I will leave you

to get ready, my Lord." He bowed and left.

"Gonna start to earn it at the party." Mikal said as he headed for the shower.

Mikal sat for a few minutes on the edge of the bed. He wanted to feel better about all of this, only he couldn't. The emotions rolling in him tore at him like a thousand claws. The anger was still there and he didn't like it. He threw the boot across the room and heard it hit the wall. He put his head in his hands and felt unreleased tears flood out of him. All the feeling of disappointment and betrayal racked him. He hated that his father didn't trust him enough to simply talk to him, to give him the decision to make. He knew he wasn't angry at Urgess or Gherrict. All of the unreleased rage was focused on Thail. He sobbed in a way he hadn't sobbed in a long time.

"Are you in that much pain, son of the house?" a slightly echoed voice asked.

Mikal raised his head and saw a glowing figure of a man. He wiped his eyes, closed them and opened them.

"I am not a hallucination, Mikal Jon Ston-Petron." the glowing man said. "Think of what you have learned, you know me."

"I'm too old to believe in fairy godfathers." Mikal said. He stared at the apparition and blinked.

"Thank you for getting my gender correct." the glowing man smiled as Mikal took a deep breath. The glowing man stood tall and strong, his eyes still bright and focused. He smiled and it made the craggy handsome face soften a bit. The hair was silver with age. Mikal knew it had to be one of the ancestri, one of his predecessors in his bloodline. He stared hard at the man and felt a comfort, strength and toughness; there seemed to be gentleness in the mix of traits. Mikal allowed himself to open to the experience, allowed the feeling to flow and felt power as well envelope him. "Do you know me, son of the house?" asked the glowing man who raised a hand to touch him.

Mikal wanted to draw back, but something inside refused retreat. He raised his hand and felt the power of an unswerving love touch him.

"I am the first who carried the name Petron. Remember your lessons; open your heart and soul."

"You're dead," Mikal said.

"I live within you, Jon. I am memory, I am in your very soul."

Mikal stepped back. He felt the wall at his back and everything was running wild in his mind. He could see the glowing man and accept that he was real. All the things he believed were playing in his mind. Could he reconcile it all and find a measure of peace with it? Mikal slipped to the floor and looked at the carpet.

"Is it that difficult to accept me?" asked the glowing man.

"Where I'm from the dead stay dead," Mikal said, "we don't usually talk to them like this."

The glowing man smiled. "I understand. It will be difficult to deal with these things. However, you are allowed to know me and all those who have gone before you. Your purpose is to save a world, not to reject it. Accept us Jon, and begin."

"Who are you?" asked Mikal.

"I am Mallot al-Petron, he who brought together the warring tribes of Schaetra and Kostrea into the house of Petron. Other houses have ruled but we have always been at the forefront even when we haven't been on the seat of power. You are an heir of that power, and you are a manifestation of it." The glowing man said. "Your acceptance of your then unborn son gave you a strength you are as yet unaware of. It allowed you to tap into us."

Mikal stared and thought about it. There were times he felt a second wind when he was at bottom emotionally. He looked up at Mallot and knew the glowing man told the truth. Why else did they celebrate when they took him and accepted him? The act of raising his son gave him a power that Thail was missing, an act of love so simple and profound it ripped through the ancestri with joy. It didn't erase years of neglect, but it was the start of the erosion, the crumbling of the wall between the two men. That he struck his father was proof of that.

"Mikal, your actions on behalf of your child were key. Your father knew he needed you when you accepted Ralton with a whole heart. The watch kept on you to let him know what sort of person you truly were." Mallot said. "Child of my house, we are in danger of losing the throne again. It may be centuries before we get it again. Thail must help the beginning of the healing process for Aboria. Jatis and Brok were a failure because they brought nothing with them that could give the strength to go on. There was nothing to fight for." He looked away at something and he bowed. Mikal knew he somehow was conferring with the ancestri. Mallot looked at Mikal again. "Commune with me child, let us strengthen you. If Thail cannot correct the downward spiral of his people, his world could very well die from the rioting. The internal decay is so great that the crown can no longer ignore it or let it slide."

"It's still not my problem." Mikal said. Mallot saw the defiance was weak and he wasn't sure what to do.

Mallot had one last card to play. "Mikal, no matter what happens, the blow you gave your father signaled to all everything has changed. Thail cannot afford to punish you as you should be. To strike him was an affront to all Aborians."

"Then why are you asking me to do this?" asked Mikal. "I don't know if I can do this!"

Mallot smiled. "We know you can. When you took custody of your child, you shared your gifts. Your love for him is great enough to allow him to develop as he will. Mikal, you demanded your father's respect when you struck him. That one blow reminded him that you are not a tool to be used at his whim." He let Mikal absorb what he just said. "Jon, I call you Jon. Commune with us. Let us help you."

Mikal stood and took a shaky step toward Mallot. He knew the spirit of this first ancestor was letting him make the decision to go all the way and accept what they had to offer. The power of knowledge and acceptance. He thought about Ralton and his life so far and knew his son would be a part of this as well. He could see a dim version of his mother in the mix of shadowy figures that surround Mallot. His Terran ancestors were part of the mix of course and Mikal could feel them calling him to the gathering of shared love and strength. The indecision and resentment were fading as he stepped forward. He held out his hands. "My heart and soul are with you ancestor, be with me."

Their hands touched and it all flooded into him, electric and powerful. He could see and feel what they felt in their lives and they knew him. Gherrict's teachings were a mere hint of what he gained now and it drove him to his knees. It was sweet, harsh, and bitter. He was drenched with sweat that cascaded down his face and ruined his new clothes. The exhaustion was exquisite. Mikal felt both energized and completely wrung out. He let go of Mallot's hands and looked up. He could see them all clearly now and he knew who they were. "Oh, wow!" Mikal breathed, "You are beautiful." The smile he wore at seeing them was augmented with tears of joy. "I didn't know I carried all of you with me."

Sandra came to him and said, "Baby, we all do. Only you get to see us."

Ralton, stopped short as he played and said "WHOA!" as what his father went through was shared with him. He could only stand and felt a bliss he'd never known. He, through his father, communed with their shared past. Ralton as the next could see his own father as both present and ancestor. "Wow, dad, this is a trip and a half."

The other children could see something was happening to Ralton. Those who achieved their ancestri knew what it was and understood this moment. Those that hadn't yet could only see the tears of joy on his face and wondered if it would be like that for them.

"Ma, how?" asked Mikal.

"First thing I learned was don't ask." Sandra said. "We can advise and guide you, but you still have to live your lives as best you can. I have always been proud of you baby." She caressed his face and Mikal thought he would die from the sheer joy of it. He felt all of them touch him and it washed over him with gentle caressing warmth.

His legs were still shaky as he tried to stand up. Mikal stumbled back and then forced himself to his feet. "I better get ready."

"You should." Mallot agreed. "Jon, you should apologize. If you are to do anything at all, anything, apologize to Thail. It does not mean you have forgiven him, it means you have decided to deal with it in a more constructive way."

Mikal gave him a "who are you kidding" look.

"Believe me, if you apologize, you will remove most of the stigma from your act."

"Most of the stigma?" asked Mikal.

"Boy, what do you want?" asked Sandra, "You're finally meeting your father, you get to go to another world and you and your son are still together. An apology isn't going to cost you that much and you are going to gain that much more when you do it."

"Even dead you're still a lawyer." Mikal said. He laughed. "All right, all right, I'll do it and try not to choke when I say it."

"You'd better!" Sandra said. She shook her head sadly.

"What's wrong?" asked Mikal as he removed his soaking shirt.

"When I joined the ancestri, they told me what Thail had in mind. It bothered me until I saw what was going on. Mike, you don't have to do this, but I want you to think about something."

"What?"

"When a man has a challenge before him, he has to choose. Tonight, you're going to meet half the problem, the nobles. The other half, the half-breeds you'll meet later. Mike, I want you to try and do something, anything you can to get some breathing room for these people."

"You believe in what he's doing, don't you?" asked Mikal. "You really did love him, didn't you?"

Sandra nodded. "He encouraged me back in the day. Mike, he's a good man despite everything he has and hasn't done. He needs you."

"I needed him too. He wasn't there when I was growing up no matter what his people did for me on his behalf. He didn't have the right."

"Then tell him that when you see him and don't let any of the nobles think they get away with anything. You are the only one to do anything about it." Sandra told him. The ancestri stood and watched the mother and son. They could see Mikal's reluctance and they knew that Sandra had to convince her son. One of the ancestri came forward. He was a dignified looking man with gray-white hair and a long beard.

"Son of the house, it is wrong what the young king has done. It can be just as wrong if you cannot begin on the road to forgiving him."

Mikal looked at Mallot, his mother and this newly known ancestor. "Now that I've accepted all of you, this means you get to tag team me, doesn't it?"

Mallot looked at Sandra. She whispered in his ear. Mikal knew she just explained what he said. Mallot looked delighted and said, "Yes it does."

"I am so outnumbered." Mikal said. He gave a rueful smile. "Oh all right." He sighed. "I'll apologize." He looked at Mallot. "Does this mean I'm a mystic like Gherrict?"

"Not quite. You're just beginning your journey." Mallot

said.

"I can't begin until I apologize to Thail, can I?" asked Mikal.

The gathered ancestri collectively nodded their heads.

Mikal considered something. "So any time I try to tap into the ancestri, it would be blocked because I hadn't set things right between the two of us."

Again they nodded.

Mikal now understood. They wanted him with the unfettered ability to commune with them. Any resentment Mikal had against his father would work against him and he could be lost to the ancestri. Mikal slowly nodded his head. This was more important. He bowed his head. The ancestri smiled knowing he was ready to do what he had to do no matter what.

CHAPTER SEVEN

THE PARTY'S ONLY BEGUN

Mikal showered and dressed again. Mallot was still in the other room although the other ancestri were gone as Mikal entered.

"Child, I have a favor to ask of you."

Mikal looked up and saw Mallot in the mirror with his reflection. He also saw that his hair was now a loose curl instead of his tight kinky hair. Mikal had to tear his eyes off the change and bring his attention to his ancestor. "Uh, I'm sorry what were you asking?"

Mallot stifled his amusement. "When you get the chance help Jatis and Brok, give them the ancestri. They were never allowed to think for themselves and they paid the cost of that. Touch them with the knowledge, please."

"I will." He looked down for a moment. Mallot took it as a bow. "I want you to know I can't call Thail 'father' yet. I still need to sort it out." Mikal said. "But, I'm glad I let you in."

"As am I, Jon." Mallot faded from sight. He looked into

the mirror and saw an elaborately carved box on the table next to him. He turned and picked it up and opened it. In it were parchment scrolls with the names of all his ancestors. He smiled and nodded knowing it was a keepsake. His name would be added to the roster when he passed from this world to the next.

Mikal looked into the mirror again. His hair went from its tight curl to a looser, more relaxed state. He had the feeling that this was a permanent change in him signifying his acceptance by the ancestri. He picked up the bow tie from the table and started tying it on, or rather, attempting to tie it on. He never wore one of these sorts of formal ties (it was a flat type meant to lay on his neck). He wanted to give up and contemplated chucking the whole thing. From the clothes he now wore, Mikal knew this was a very formal affair. Everything had to be in place and the suit of clothes was testament to that. A deep blue jacket and pants with fine silver trim. The jacket was a swallow tail cut, very fine and body conscious. The pants seemed to flow on him like water. Back on Earth he never bought into sagging his pants, although he wore clothes that were loose and comfortable and he could move in them, these clothes felt like he wore nothing at all. The shirt had a ruffle of fine lace at the wrists and was a fine silk that shimmered in the light. His boots were of polished black leather from some kind of lizard and the scales shimmered as well. There were cuff links with diamonds and a ring of white gold that had a double ring symbol of some type. Mikal thought it was a symbol of his being a half-breed and the rings were of two worlds.

As Mikal examined the cuff links, the Queen appeared at his room door. "Forgive me, Your Majesty. I didn't hear you come in."

"I suppose you wouldn't." Uasar said, amused. "The cuff links are most beautiful."

Mikal could feel the blush. "I thought they and the ring were interesting, that's all."

"Of course," Uasar said as she approached him. "Please, turn around and let us have a look at you." Mikal did as he was told feeling like one of the aunts he liked back on Earth was inspecting him before an important family event. "Very, very good. You shall be quite presentable tonight."

"I would think you wouldn't be happy with me after what I did today. As a matter of fact, I thought this whole thing would be called off by now." Mikal said.

"Our problem is, you should be punished. Our other problem is, you were right." The Queen was frank; "your father mishandled this from the start."

Mikal turned and faced her and let the tie hang there. "You think I'm right?!"

Uasar smiled in a way that reminded Mikal of his mother. That same knowing how the situation was and knowing how to deal with it that shocked him no matter how many times he saw it. "You had a life and a son. Thail did not do the one thing that he should have done and that's talk to you. I have no doubt if you knew about your father you would consider coming with us. On the other hand, he is our king, he has every right to kill you for striking him. No one would say anything about it."

"Then I'm glad I got my shot in." Mikal said. "Damn this tie!" He threw it on the dresser in disgust.

Uasar came over to him and picked the tie up. She turned him to face her and proceeded to put the tie on him perfectly.

Mikal looked in the mirror. "I guess you guys have dressers helping you to get ready?"

"They help." Uasar went to the bed and sat down. "I'm sure there was no protocol training on your birth world. Gherrict's very good about a lot of things, but sometimes he just doesn't care about the niceties."

"Actually, he did manage to instruct me." Mikal said. "That's why I'm standing."

"So you are. I know he will continue your instruction on the way." Uasar said. "Jon, we must ask you to apologize to your father. It will not take the stain away, but you must do so. There will be considerably more difficulty for you if you don't. For you to have struck your father undermined his credibility and threw doubt on the validity of bringing you to Aboria. I'm sure Gherrict told you about the two before you, Jatis and Brok?"

"Yes, he did."

"Good. I want you to know there are more than a few

who agreed with your actions; Thail endangers your son's life and cost you the one you were building." Uasar looked at him directly. Mikal could feel the steel in the queen and there was no messing around with her. That too was like his mother. "Thail is not an evil or bad man. He is one of many full bloods who forgot their children. They forget those children also do without them." She appraised Mikal without condescension. Mikal could sense she was genuinely concerned about what he was going through.

"Mikal, you must understand. Nearly thirty percent of our population is now half-breed. We have written laws, some of them very foolish, which have disenfranchised these children. The trouble is, these children are starting to awake and their actions are going to change us. What is needed is a strong voice. Tonight at the table, you will be attacked viciously. This is no fault of your own. It was going to happen. Many of the lords do not want the necessary changes to be made. Those changes are happening as we speak."

Mikal looked at her. "Then why do you need me?"

Thail rubbed his arm. It wasn't as sore now and he felt like he could make it an evening. He looked in the mirror and wondered about this son of his Terran woman. Damn it, the boy struck him!

It galled, frankly. Thail wanted to have the boy taken apart, but he needed him. There was also the question of this new grandson. Thail knew the child was his father's son and

Thail the stranger. He ruefully chuckled to himself. Gherrict and Urgess knew them better than he did.

It was hard to admit that this one was a fighter and determined to have the best life for him and his son. It was hard to admit all of that.

Why was that hard? All fathers wanted the same thing for their children, their happiness. Mikal was doing his best when Thail had him taken from his world. Jatis and Brok were the same. The difference was simple. Jatis and Brok were younger, more vulnerable. They did not have the ancestri. Mikal was tested in so many ways, not the least being fatherhood.

Thail looked up and saw himself in the mirror. What had tested him? He'd spent much of his time running away from his duties and responsibilities and took them on with great reluctance. Mikal faced his head on and won his right to be a man. Suddenly, the hollow feeling was back and Thail didn't feel right. The pit gnawing in his stomach seemed to rip a great hole in him and he wanted to scream out. Thail never got the ancestri. The blood knowledge was not his. If Mikal had gotten it before he came to the ship, it meant he had every right to strike him, every right to tell him off.

The cold sweat that drenched him was back.

"Unlike Thail, I have read some of your stories. Whatever you may say of yourself, you have strong beliefs and a strong point of view."

Mikal cocked an eyebrow. "Aren't they the same?"

"Not really." Uasar continued. "You might have one but not the other. You have acted on your beliefs and your point of view is based on those beliefs. You are going to have to speak out tonight and define and defend yourself. Believe me when I say the blood on the floor should not only be yours; the lords should be soaking in it by the evening's end."

"You want me to do the same to them as I did Thail?"

"Yes. They must know the future goes with the half-breeds whether they like it or not." Uasar said.

"What's your stake in it your majesty?" Mikal asked. "You're not doing this out of a love for your husband. The man has stepped out on you."

"You're quite right. I do it for the love of my world and my people." Uasar said. "We have betrayed ourselves, Mikal. We have made children we have chosen to be ashamed of instead of embracing them. Our cousins the Vichar have said a drop of Vicharian blood makes you Vicharian. They take their children's strength into themselves and become stronger. We have become weaker with our divided house. It collapses all around us and no one sees it."

"I tell you what I told Gherrict. I'm no messiah." Mikal said.

"No, you are not." Uasar sat silent for a moment. "Your mother was beautiful, I'm told."

"She was." Mikal went to a suitcase and pulled out the photo album. He pulled a picture of Sandra and Thail from it and handed it over to Uasar. She took it and examined it.

"I can understand why he fell for her. He always did have an eye for beauty."

"You're not jealous?"

"I'm suppose I'm used to Thail having had so many lovers. I suppose it's like the furniture, always there and you don't notice it until you need to find a seat."

Mikal broke up laughing until tears came from his eyes. He wiped and stared at Uasar for a moment. She handed him the photo back. Mikal put it back into the album. "Okay, mistresses as furniture; that one will be in my head for awhile." He put the album back in the suitcase and put the suitcase in the closet. "Your majesty, where would you like the new mistress placed? (He dropped his voice) In the corner, and get a doily, the queen must not notice her!"

Uasar could barely keep her laughter and she gave up letting the peal of laughter out. "That is silly!"

Mikal continued. "I can just see it now. You come into the mistress room and rearrange all of them! 'That older one in the hallway must be replaced, and style the hair on the one in the bedroom, it's out of fashion now!'"

"Stop it!" Uasar said. "It would never happen that way and you know it! I'm very good friends with all of my husband's former lovers."

"I heard, Gherrict told me." Mikal said as he settled down. "I think it shows a lot of class to do what you've done for them."

"It was necessary, Jon." Uasar sobered up. "Their needs had to be met, and there was no one else. I keep in touch, I help out and they have better lives because of it. I wanted them to know at least one Aborian with honor."

"Mom would have liked you." Mikal said as he placed a kiss on her cheek. "I hope I wasn't too forward."

"Not at all," she said as she returned the kiss. "It's time we left for the party." She stood and went to the mirror and checked herself. "There are really only four of these affairs you should do. The rest is simply tedium. I will have to point out the royals who really count and make sure you get to know them."

"Meet all the right people." Mikal said.

"On Abor, you are who you know, remember that. The politics you now begin to play have a great deal of family histories behind them. Right now, you are the wild card." Uasar turned to him. "Consider your words carefully, Jon. What you said to your father in the docking bay is being discussed by everyone, from the servants to the royals. That is why the physical blow you struck must be apologized for, but not the words. You spoke the truth."

"And the truth shall set you free." Mikal said. He slipped on the jacket.

Uasar nodded in approval. "Very good, you shall make an excellent second impression."

"First one was pretty bad, wasn't it?" Mikal said as he left the room after her.

"It was a bitch, Jon." Uasar surprised him.

Mikal smiled and followed her and the servants to the party.

He passed through the amphitheater when he was put in the cooling off room and Mikal thought it would look awesome when it was setup for a party. He was right. It was jaw dropping spectacular. He didn't know where to look first. There were dancers on wires above their heads. An orchestra played intense, beautiful music that Mikal might have called classical. He wanted to look at everything and he couldn't see everything. Mikal decided to people watch.

The clothes were so incredible, they made any Academy Awards pre-show look like an appeal for the poor. Women wore gossamer fabrics and jewelry so exquisite, Mikal wondered at the skill involved in its creation. Diamonds and gems of every color draped necks, wrists and ears in dazzling arrays of glittering perfection. Mikal felt under dressed.

Drawing in a breath, he spotted Thail standing at the head table. The king wore expertly tailored clothing that accented his natural grace and physique. It may as well be painted on. Uasar didn't miss a step. She was gorgeous in a deep green dress that moved on her like flowing water. She looked like a supermodel, thought Mikal. With her heart-shaped face and five foot seven frame, the queen was a stunner. Mikal knew she was sure of herself and her power. Despite Thail's actions, she enjoyed her position. Uasar saw to her husband's paramours and gained valuable allies through her marriage.

She knew how to use the leverage she possessed.

Thail looked the part of a king. For Mikal it made it harder to accept this man as a father, let alone his. This was flesh of his flesh and perhaps it would take time to see him as such.

Thail turned and spotted Uasar and Mikal as they approached the head table. Thail and Uasar embraced as Ralton joined them. The father and son stared at each other for a moment. Anger was in Thail's eyes and it matched his son's resentment. Both were gently steered to their seats and Mikal and Ralton sat down after the king and queen did.

Thail tapped his glass and the room quieted down. He stood up and said "Tonight, we welcome a son. Tonight, we begin the journey to his new life on Abor. This is our first meal together and as you all know, firsts are difficult things." There was some low tittering as he looked at Mikal. "We have a small idea of who he is. He has no idea who we are. Therefore, we have made an error in judgment in the manner we brought him here. It is not how a child should be treated. Our error was that we did not respect who he was at the moment, we did not value the life he was leading. We shall not make that mistake again, and we ask him for his forgiveness."

Mikal tried to swallow his surprise. Kings didn't do this, did they? Thail just put the ball squarely back in his son's court and now Mikal had to say something. Mikal stood and looked at Thail while trying to keep the surprise off his face. "I have known what His Majesty looked like. My mother had images of him, so I knew of him." The crowd noticed Mikal did not say father. "I, too ask for forgiveness for the blows I struck, but not for my words. To me, a king sets the pace. What was done took something from me you should not have taken. My joy at knowing who I am has been dimmed. I would have come with you gladly if you had only asked." He spread his arms out and turned around and laughed. "You don't know how I've dreamed of something like this! The very fact that someone from another world is my father. You don't know, you just don't know how much this means to me. What was a fantasy is now a reality." The crowd stared at him as he explained. "To know your world's blood flows through me, wow!" He faced Thail squarely. "Perhaps many here, they will think me a hopeless romantic or a fool. I can live with that. I can't live with what His Majesty did to get me here. I want it right between us. I want us both to remember there are lines that just shouldn't be crossed." He held out his hand. "I am sorry sir." Thail took it and shook it to applause. It was a start.

Thail bid Mikal to sit down, amazed at what was just done. Mikal managed to apologize, explain himself and still reinforce what he said all at the same time. Perhaps there were depths to this son he didn't suspect. Mikal stopped a lot of trouble by apologizing. He also set himself up as someone to watch carefully since you couldn't tell how he would move. Thail now understood these were the same traits Mikal's mother had . Thail was now sure he was right about bringing his son home.

For Mikal's part, he knew he just killed a lot of "you struck my king" nonsense. No matter what, Mikal's point of view was American. He didn't really care if Thail was a king. The real changes to come were from the bottom up, not the top down.

CHAPTER EIGHT

A TOUCH FOR A TOUCH

The food was being served. The royal table was served first. Mikal watched as the many servants moved surely through the tables. Ralt was watching them as well and looked up to his father.

"They know what they are doing, don't they Dad?" asked Ralt.

"They had better. They represent the royal family in their duties." Mikal said. "Every one of the servants has to be the best."

"I bet they practice." Ralt surmised.

"I know they practice. That's the only way they can be so good." his father said as a beautiful plate of food was set before him. He inhaled deeply and was rewarded with a rush of fragrance. He'd never smelled the like and he closed his eyes and let the sensation fill him.

The queen watched with amusement. "That wondrous, Mikal?"

"What can I say, Majesty? You eat with your senses."

Mikal said as he took up the knife and fork. "Right now, I am feasting."

"I'm sure the chef will approve." Uasar told him. She turned to Ralt. "How is your meal, young Ralton?"

Ralt swallowed, surprised. "It's very good. I've never tasted anything like this."

"You should expect such meals in the palace, my dear." The queen said. "We have very good chefs there and we are very lucky that they choose to work for us."

"I would think he'd want to work at the palace since it means he's got one of the best jobs 'cause you only hire the best." Ralt said. "I mean, you can't settle for anything less than the best."

"Quite right, Ralton," The queen said. "It would not do to settle for less than the best." She looked at her husband and saw the glance he gave to Mikal. She wondered what he thought of this son now. Mikal made the apology. Was he still smarting from the blow that put him on the floor? Uasar could feel it in her bones that the blow needed to be accounted for. The king could ill afford to not answer the affront to him. There had to be some kind of satisfactory resolution out of all of this. She looked over at Mikal who took the glances at his father only when the king wasn't looking. Uasar wondered now what went through Mikal's mind as he stole looks at his father. She knew she couldn't be the only one who noticed. She let her eyes roam over the crowd. On the level they sat, the royal table was clearly seen from every angle in the huge room. Uasar could see the whispered conversations about them, and could see Ralton fidget in his seat.

Ralt kept his eyes on his plate ignoring the attention. Uasar could see him trying to fight back tears. The unspoken and unresolved tension between father and son was affecting him and he couldn't say.

"Ralton, would you like to leave?" Uasar whispered to him.

Ralt shook his head no, knowing if he left it would make things worse. He had to stick it out. He was glad the next course was served as it allowed him to not think about it for a moment. He looked at the queen. "This looks really good."

"It's quite good, my dear." Uasar said. "I think you will like it. I am quite pleased you are willing to try new things."

"Back home, I had to try new things. I never knew what we were gonna get to eat sometimes," Ralton explained, "So a lot of things we got were new to me."

"You were poor?" asked Uasar.

"Compared to this yeah. We were on public assistance for a long time before my dad found a job." Ralton told her. "A lot of times we got surplus food. Some of it was really good, though." He speared some of the salad on his fork and lifted it to his mouth.

Uasar thought about it. It made sense. Mikal fought for what he got. That would make a difference. "Tell me, didn't you have relatives you could stay with?"

Ralt rolled his eyes. "Yeah, we could stay with them if you didn't mind putting up with their stuff."

Uasar could hear Ralt changed what he was going to say. Was it so bad they couldn't stay with their family? She wondered. "Was your family not accommodating?"

"Yeah, we could stay only if we had the money. My great-aunt hated my dad. She even hated his father. She charged us rent and wouldn't let my dad have the money my grandmother left him. As a matter of fact, she spent it and dad couldn't do anything about it. When he threatened to sue, she told him it went to his room and board. That was a lie, she charged him four hundred a month to stay in the garage. She would park her car in there when we went out and told us to wait until she was ready to take it out. I hated her."

"Was there no one else you could turn to?" asked a horrified Uasar. "It could not have been completely bad."

"My dad got a van and we lived in that for awhile." Ralt said. "When we left Earth, we had lived in that apartment for only six months. It was all coming together and we could have most of we wanted and had just about everything we needed." He sighed. "I don't think the king can ever understand what it means to have what you needed and wanted in your grasp and then have someone take it all away." He looked at her. "It hurt. I saw my dad cry for the first time. I went in my room because I didn't want him to see me crying too."

She would have held him right then but she held off. It wouldn't do here. Uasar understood Mikal a little better now knowing the blow was for all the damage caused. Knowing that, she was now more willing to excuse Mikal reminding Thail, the entire ship, that such a thing as a man's life was important if only to the man living it. They had to exorcise this demon and soon. If Thail was honest with himself, he and Mikal had to make it a fair fight this time. they had to know the blows were coming.

Uasar knew how Mikal's mother had died. It was horrible for Sandra to be dragged behind the car of a drunk driver. When the man finally was stopped, he laughed when he heard what was done. Mikal must have received some satisfaction knowing the man was a three time loser and was in prison for life. Sandra's sister Bertha gave a great performance in court when she let the man know how the family hurt over this.

Bertha got control of Sandra's estate. She saw to it Joe, Stephanie and Jennifer got some of what their mother left them. Mikal saw none of the money that was supposed to come to him. With the exception of the school fund in his name, Bertha cut him off completely. "You're lucky I let you stay in this house," she told him when he protested.

Mikal's only real action was to do better in school. He wanted to do well so he could leave the house owing Bertha nothing.

Mikal also spent his time earning pocket money. He worked hard and got the video camera and equipment he wanted to make amateur video productions. He did the special effects on super eight films until he couldn't get that format any more. He even learned to sew his own clothes and make costumes. He also lifted weights and learned to defend himself at school. When Ralt came into his life, he managed to keep a lot of what he built up over the years. He taught himself to read and write music so he could write the score to his videos and films.

So much work, so much effort now gone because of a father he didn't know.

Uasar knew the blow was for more than just the job. It was for everything. Thail now owed Mikal. Could Thail give Mikal the opportunity to do well here and find his way with little interference? That was the question, wasn't it?

Uasar knew they had to get through the mutual resentment and anger that had them.

Uasar's own feelings were what they were. She understood she wasn't enough, nor were any number of women enough for Thail. Still, she knew his former lovers and had a good information on whom was he sleeping with these days. Knowing the man had no compunction to remain faithful, she married Thail. Ten children in his marriage and he still sought other women! Uasar would have been insulted except her position gave her the upper hand over those other women. She was Queen and that position had power and prestige no matter how her husband acted. She would not give it up for any reason. Thail on the other hand, even if he didn't admit it, knew he was a piss poor husband to his long-suffering wife. His children knew what their father was doing and it reflected badly on him. Uasar looked all the more honorable by not taking the lovers she would be justified in having.

Soon enough, the meal was finished and the real feasting would begin.

Mikal sat at the table after everyone else got up to mingle around. He somehow couldn't force himself to stand up, and watched the royal in their finery begin their conversations in earnest, positioning themselves for the night. They all knew that Mikal would begin to make his way through the crowd. The elders made sure their children had the first time with him. Mikal wondered how sharp their claws were.

Finally, Mikal stood and made his way to the level Uasar pointed out to him. He looked up and saw the younger royals. Although he was twenty-seven years old Earth time, he was only about four years old by the Aborian calendar. He couldn't imagine a year with eleven hundred and ten point three six eight days. It had twelve months but those months were ninety-two point five three days apiece. With thirty-hour days, Mikal and Ralton faced a total rethinking on their relationship with time.

As he made the top of the stairs, Mikal heard, "All hail the new prince! He graces us with his presence!" The speaker was a medium build youth with dark auburn hair, deep green eyes and high cheekbones. He wore a deep gold suit with matching boots and a small waist length fur trimmed cape and several rings on both fingers. Mikal thought he had a flamboyant manner that perfectly suited him. The young lady who sat next to him wore a slinky number of matching gold and pumps on sheer gold stocking feet. Her hair was big and full, gathered in a coiled ponytail.

"Be fair, Ronal! He is new to us, true, but he is also a member of our select group." She said.

"My dear Cayla, I would never deny that. But, we must remember that he did strike our most honorable king." Ronal said. "Perhaps he might tell us how he would have his father act?"

Mikal looked at the two and then the others. He gave a small shrug and took a glass of the excellent sparkling wine from the passing tray. "Perhaps you think he was right in doing what he did?" He took a drink from the glass. Normally, he didn't drink. Tonight he thought he might need the help.

Cayla twirled her glass in her fingers slowly. "Perhaps the new prince believes his rights are more important than his majesty's needs?"

Mikal swirled the sip he just took in his mouth and swallowed. "I supposed you have no idea how much I valued the life I led. I also suppose you don't think that if he could do that to me, what might he do to you?" He looked at her with an amused gaze. "I don't know how it is here. All I know is that in my home land, we overthrew a king we disagreed with and started the country."

Cayla looked around with great amusement. "Did you not hear, my friends? He lives in a country that was started by rebellion!" She wore a look of great amusement. "Why one might think he would lead a rebellion against the king!"

Mikal mentally counted to ten. "I hate to say this, but you would be among the first to go."

That wiped the smirk off Cayla's face. "You would kill all of us?"

Mikal nodded. "It is obvious that you are part of the problem. You don't respect anyone."

Cayla was taken aback. "I respect my inferiors!"

Mikal couldn't resist. "Where do you find them?"

Cayla was slack jawed.

"Do you respect the people that do all the work so you can live your life?" Mikal asked. "Have you ever prepared a meal? Taken care of your own laundry? I mean, you can't say the people who do your glorious hair and fabulous dresses and perfect makeup earn your respect, do they?"

The other young royals stifled their comments. Mikal did have a point.

Ronal broke the uncomfortable silence after looking at his companions and realizing Mikal did not fear them no matter how much they thought he should. "Are you saying we don't see our helpers?"

"Is that what you call them?" asked Mikal.

"Well, they do help. I don't think that our

preoccupation with other things means we don't appreciate them." Ronal said. "After all, they do help us do our jobs."

Mikal shrugged. "I suppose. These guys work hard to make you look good. I have to wonder if you appreciate all they do."

"I know I do." Ronal said defensively. "We see the things they do and acknowledge them. They are compensated fairly and their needs are taken care of. You cannot ask for more than that."

"Like I said, how about respect?" Mikal asked. "Just everyday plain old respect, the real kind that lets them know their work is appreciated. Are they treated with what you demand?"

"Why are you concerned about servants?" another asked. "Is it because you are no more than they are?"

Mikal smiled. "No, I just think you should be careful. After all, it's usually the servants that know where to take you out of the picture should a rebellion ever start up and they decide to take their frustrations out on you. You have no idea of what someone may think even if you believe you have control of the situation."

Another woman, Halona asked, "Do you think we are not careful how we deal with our servants? Do you wish a rebellion on us?"

Mikal took a sip. "No, I was just wondering."

Halona was astonished. "How could you say such things?! We are not evil!"

"I didn't say you are. All I asked was how you feel about the servants. After all, if I am no better than they are, I don't think you can respect me. All you will ever see is a servant that needs to be punished, not an equal." He took another sip from his glass.

The others looked at each other not knowing what to think. They saw this new prince strike his father over how he was brought here. What they couldn't understand was why couldn't he just accept what was done? They believed Mikal was going to a better world. Yet Mikal didn't see it that way. He saw them closer to enemies than friends. Halona could only think that the rift between father and son had to be healed. Halona looked over at her companion who asked the next question.

"Do you believe the king had no right to do what he did?" he asked. "A king must be allowed greater latitude in his dealings."

"True, but that same latitude could end up getting people killed." Mikal said. "How that king handles latitude is as important as what he must deal with."

"Are you saying that the king should not have that latitude?" he asked.

"No, I'm simply saying he should be careful how he handles it. A wrong move could be disastrous," replied Mikal.

His questioner nodded in agreement. "Still, he is king."

"That doesn't excuse him from simple respect." Mikal said. "I can forgive him. Until the hurt goes away it will be difficult." He looked them in the eyes. "I understand you being on his side. Like you said, he is king. But he is my father and I expected better from him."

"You're that disappointed?" asked Cayla. "I had no idea."

"I don't think he does, either." Mikal put his glass down. "I guess I just was hoping he respected my mother's memory enough to talk to their son." He looked at the floor as the others stared at him.

"Were your expectations that high?" asked Halona.

"Yeah," Mikal said. "I never thought he would hide behind his title and position when he came to get me."

"That is not fair!" Cayla said. "The king has every right to do what he thinks is correct!"

"So he had the right to destroy a reputation? I know for you, it doesn't matter, but for me it is important to be able to have my word mean something. If I couldn't have my word believed what would be the point?"

"You raise a point, Ston-Petron." Another youth said.

"Would you mind identifying yourself? I don't like not having a name to go with a speaker." Mikal said.

He smiled. "Very well, then. My name is Viscount Garrin Daulcour. I simply wonder if it isn't all just a result of your being a half-breed." He looked at his companions. "After all, being a half-breed puts you in a precarious position. Your rights are proscribed, you really only can serve in the armed forces and you are taxed at a greater rate than most full-bloods. I must wonder if you aren't fighting your father because you might not believe he has the right to demand of you."

Mikal looked at the scene below him. "Demand of me?"

Daulcour took a sip from his glass. "Demand of you service you may feel he has no right to. It is a difficult thing to be asked to be a, well, for lack of a better word, a savior. You are being asked to take care of a group of people you know nothing about. It would be daunting for any one."

Mikal raised an eyebrow. Daulcour had a point. He was being asked to take care of people he didn't know. The task loomed large in front of him and he didn't know if he could do it. Noticing a half-breed servant passing below. Mikal watched as the man moved anonymously through the crowd carrying his tray of drinks. It was impressive how he managed to keep his balance, not touch the royals, and make sure they got their drinks.

Mikal looked at Daulcour. "Come here." Daulcour moved close and Mikal pointed to the man serving drinks. "Do you see what he's doing? He is doing his job." He looked at Daulcour. "He's keeping out of trouble, keeping his balance and making sure you and I are being served. That's what we are, servants, making sure that everyone has a shot at doing their best."

"That is an unusual way of putting it." Daulcour said.

"Think about it. Keeping them safe from our enemies, allow them to build their money. The job is to make sure all our people are the best they can be." Mikal said. "We diminish ourselves and our people by failing to allow for all the possibilities." He took a sip from his glass. "Is that what you want?"

Daulcour saw Mikal was serious. "You think that half-breeds are capable of great things?"

Mikal smiled. "If I didn't, I wouldn't be telling you about it." He drained his glass. "I need to make arrangement to talk to some half-breeds. In order to know what they're thinking, I shouldn't be talking to you. Besides, do you know what it truly means to be a half-breed? It means you have multiple heritages. Thanks to some of your elders, most half-breeds can't celebrate it." Daulcour watched as Mikal put the glass down and left their company, realizing Mikal really didn't need them, regarding them as unnecessary obstacles.

Daulcour turned to his companions. "Well, my friends, it seems we have a half-breed with very little real use for us."

Cayla moved slowly to her friend. "I think he's going to be all right. He knows who he is."

Ronal watched as Mikal made his way down to his son. He understood what his friends were realizing; no matter how Mikal protested his getting here, he was willing to take on the job. "Do you think he'll succeed?"

Cayla took a drink. "It is possible. My question is what will he do about how his sector is going to be financed? They haven't received an increase in some twenty standard years. He's going to have to find financing."

"That, I wouldn't worry about." Ronal said. "He will find a way around it." He pressed a button on his lapel and said: "Did you hear that father?"

Ronal father's voice came over the small hidden listening device. "Yes, my son. It was interesting. He told you everything and nothing."

"How do you mean?"

"Mikal has to investigate what life is like for half-breeds, in order know what they think."

"Interesting. Mikal doesn't seem like the sort to formulate a plan without knowing what he faces."

"This is true. That makes him dangerous." The voice said. "The trick will be to wait and see his next move. I take it he's done with you?"

"Yes father. I also believe that he sees us as obstacles." Ronal said, "We may very well be irrelevant."

"Indeed. It is my suggestion that you make friends with him for now. You have no idea what he may turn out to be. We may need him."

"He may see through it, father, he is not a fool."

"That is why you make friends with him, you don't know who you will need."

His father signed off and Ronal couldn't see Mikal anymore. He thought to himself, this may be the one if he does it right. But now, his world hung in a balance and Ronal wasn't sure if any one person could do anything. He wondered if the half-breed thought about that. Ronal could see on his friends' faces that he wasn't the only one wondering.

It would be interesting.

CHAPTER NINE

WE ALL SHINE ON

Mikal found Ralt playing with a group of youngsters in one of the video arcades two floors below. The boy sat in a high baked chair meant to look like a star fighter's chair and the simulation of the cockpit surrounded him. Ralt flew in a furious competition with another boy. Mikal's mom was right, most kids found their own level if left alone. It wasn't until the parents taught their own prejudices that many of them found it difficult to make friends. Mikal smiled and left his son alone to play with what Mikal hoped were new found friends.

Making his way to another level, he saw elder Aborians chatting with each other. They saw him and the invitation was implied. Taking another flute of sparkling wine he made his way over to them.

"Greetings, young prince," one said as he joined them. "I am Garroth Daulcour."

"Ronal Daulcour's father," Mikal said. "I was talking to your son. I suppose you heard?"

"How did you know he was wired?" asked Daulcour.

"You just told me." Mikal smiled.

Daulcour's mouth dropped open.

"Let's be honest, you want as much as you can get on me." Mikal said as he took a sip from his glass.

Daulcour roared with laughter. "Do you do this all the time?"

Mikal shrugged. "The one thing I know is that my father sent two uncles to get me. They spent time in my closet after they turned it into a massive multi roomed place. I figured you might have your kid wired so you could take my measure. I was right, wasn't I?"

Daulcour glanced at his companions. "You had no clue."

Mikal shrugged again. "I could guess."

The gathered royals shook their heads in disbelief. An elegant woman dressed in a silken blue-green dress and a small crown of diamond and pearls regarded him with amusement. "If we could have seen this, we might have had a better first impression of you."

"If I had gotten better treatment when they brought me, you might have." Mikal said. "Aboria hasn't made a good first impression on me either."

"Tell me something," the woman in the crown said, "do you believe we full-bloods have made mistakes with our half-breeds?"

"They are your sons and daughters, nephews and nieces,

brothers and sisters. They should not be excluded from the fullest participation of the world." Mikal replied. "They should be able to do everything in their power to live the best, fullest lives they can. Otherwise, everybody loses."

Another man raised an eyebrow. "Then you believe that we have limited Aboria's advance by limiting our half-breeds?"

"Attitude helps. I would think you should forget about calling them our half-breeds; you don't own them. I know you don't own me." Mikal took another sip from his flute. "I think some of the problem is a matter of how you see them. As possessions, not citizens, things not worthy of your full investment."

The royals stared at him. The woman in the crown asked, "Are you saying we have neglected the half-breeds and we deserve the troubles we have with them?" she looked at her companions. "We have done what we can for them! They don't need for anything!"

Mikal smiled. "Sure you're right."

"What does that mean?" she demanded.

"It means exactly what it means." Mikal said, cocking an eyebrow.

"If you'll excuse me, I want to go look at the bandstand. I have never seen those kinds of instruments." Mikal bowed to them and left.

Daulcour and the others watched Mikal leave. He would have sworn but he kept it to himself. Instead he said, "that one will be interesting. Do you think he will have a chance with the right sector?"

"I'll be surprised if he gets anything other than Bavos-Haim. That is our half-breed sector." One of the other men said. "The difficulty is how will he affect us? Think about it my friends, he will change us because he doesn't care about us, he cares about what happens to him and his son."

Daulcour stared at him. "Are you saying that when the king took him, Mikal saw it as a threat against his son?"

"Wouldn't you?" the man asked. "Think about it. We will do everything we can to protect our children. In that we and Mikal meet as equals."

Daulcour stared at the back of the retreating Mikal. "Gods and ancestors! The king and his son must finally meet as father and son in order to sort this out."

"Yes," the crowned woman said, "they must become father and son, or all will be lost."

Mikal saw Ralt at the bandstand as he tried a hammer harp. The boy took the felt faced hammers and struck the harp gently. He smiled at the sound and tried a few runs of the scales he recently learned. It amused the gathered crowd to no end to watch the boy discover the music in the instrument. Suddenly, he started a song. Mikal recognized it; "Instant Karma" by John Lennon. Ralt started to sing "and we all shine on," and the gathered were amazed at the power in the boy's voice. Mikal's face shone with pride as Ralt finished.

Trouble was, Arap Ma'oog the musician who owned the harp, didn't like it the half-breed youth was playing it. He leapt on the bandstand and pushed the boy down and away from the instrument. Those who knew about Mikal and his father were not surprised to see Mikal rush to the bandstand and confront Ma'oog.

"What is your problem?" Mikal demanded, "Who do you wish you were?!"

"The boy had no business playing my harp!" Ma'oog answered defiantly, "I don't allow half-breed trash to play my harp!"

The look of fury on Mikal's face told everyone Ma'oog said the wrong thing. Ma'oog didn't see the shot to his stomach. Mikal grabbed Ma'oog by the hair and slammed his face into the harp. He then brought his knee into the stomach again and again. Ma'oog fell to the floor and Mikal kicked him in the face knocking him off the bandstand. Several guards grabbed Mikal and held him as they pulled him away. "That's enough!" one of the guards said, "You made your point!"

Mikal's face was twisted and everyone gathered could see just how far he would go to protect his son. There was no doubt in many minds his son was the reason Mikal struck the king. Thail could see that clearly now from his vantage point. His life did not have the value Ralton's did for Mikal.

Ma'oog was taken away before the guards let Mikal go.

He called for Ralt to follow him to their rooms and Ralt knew enough to not give an argument and fell into step behind his father.

Ronal Daulcour looked at his companions. "Well, now we know the real reason Ston-Petron struck his father. You don't muck with his cub, that can get you killed."

"Indeed!" Cayla said before she took a drink from her glass.

Uasar watched as her husband left the gathering. She knew now what drove Mikal as much as any ambitions he might have. That single child meant more than anything her husband had to offer. Mikal could very well betray Aboria to protect his son and they had done nothing to gain his loyalty. Uasar saw to the bastards (as much she hated the word, there really was no other for them) by the other women, she felt Mikal would prove a harder case in gaining his trust. Uasar needed to talk to Gherrict and Urgess soon. They had to bring down the tension.

They were a few days away from Aboria and Mikal sat in the space the queen secured for him. His recording equipment was laid out and he was working. Ralt watched his dad play back the previously recorded tracks. Even now, there were some Aborians watching them and talking about what they were doing. The tracks were carefully built until he had what he wanted. Ralt knew his father liked all sorts of music. He knew Mikal composed a song as gospel music when he couldn't find a more pop sound he liked. Mikal also tended to compose in a more classical idiom when that didn't work. The new song felt very Bach-like with its fugue opening, the odd time changes and its gospel chorus with its call and response seem to put the odd spin on the whole. But it worked.

"Remember the girl, Alisa who helped you with the breed slang?" Mikal asked his son.

"Yeah, I liked her," replied Ralt.

"Well, this is for her." Mikal said. "Let's give it a try."

Mikal stepped to the microphone and began. His strong tenor voice started low and then began to pick up power and confidence as he went on.

"SILVER HAIRED LADY"

You've gone through so much
In a hard, hard life
The storms you faced caused you nothing but strife
But you took a stand
You faced your fears
Threw your shoulders back
And wiped away your tears
Oh, yeah
You did what you had to do

Silver Haired Lady

With a golden heart
What is there left to say?
When I was down,
You picked me up
And showed me a brand new way

Oooh, you are so strong
You are so good
If I could give a fraction back,
You know I would
Silver
Sweet Silver Haired Lady
With the gentle words that soothe my pain away . . .

Now tell me
Who do I thank for your being here?
How do you thank
Someone for the joy
They've given you

Silver Haired
Silver Haired
Sweet, Sweet
Silver Haired lady

Mikal and Ralt traded vocals, with Ralt shocking the onlookers with a surprisingly mature voice for his age. They listened to the playback and then went back and layered their vocals to create a bigger sounding group of chorus singers than they had. The gathered onlookers never saw Earth recording equipment before, primitive as it was compared to what they had on Aboria. It was surprising to hear the excellent results that they got with their equipment. As Mikal mixed it down to two tracks for stereo, Ralt made sure they got a two-track mix as he manned the other console. Mikal could make tracks that sounded deeper and richer and Ralt bobbed his head to the music. Their audience listened with appreciation as the song came together.

"Okay, I can live with it for now. I'll see how I feel about it tomorrow." Mikal said as he pulled another sheet out of his folder.

"Hey, it's for the queen!" said Ralt.

"Yeah I thought it would be nice to do something for her. I kind of like her style." Mikal told his son.

"That and the fact she told you off." quipped Ralt.

"When did you hear that?" asked Mikal.

Ralt shrugged. "It got around that you and the queen talked that night after we left the party. I overheard two guards telling another about it. They recorded you two." He smiled. "I talked them into letting me see it. They got a lot of interesting stuff on video disk."

Mikal gave his son a sour look. "Video disk, huh? Ain't that just the perfect bitch?" Ralt just shrugged again. "Anyway, here's the song. Let's just see the chord changes."

They negotiated the changes again. Mikal set up the drum track while Ralt laid his base down with him. They moved to the keyboards and guitars. It was medium tempo and the beat had an undertow that seemed to drag the listener into the song. The crowd was getting larger.

Mikal stepped to the microphone and clipped the lyric sheet to the copy board in front of him.

"LADY QUEEN"

What did I know? Nothing
What did I feel? Nothing
Until you came along
Everything was wrong
And there was nothing to feel
And there was nothing to know at all

Lady Queen
You became friend to me
You tried to make me see all the possibilities
Of the journey in front of me
You turned it around, around
You turned it around for me

I admit
I was scared

Thinking no one here really cared
But you held a mirror to me
And made me see the reflections I didn't want to see
A father I don't know
And who doesn't know me
The stands we each took
Was destroying him and me

Lady Queen
How did you see?
The unrealized possibilities
The things we didn't want to see
In the unrealized him and me?

You're seeing the two of us
In the ways we don't want to see

Here Mikal allowed the bridge to soar letting the music speak in the way the words could not. He made the guitar a little louder and brought the synthesized strings out a little more. He looked up and saw a man shaking his head in disagreement. Obviously, he thought something was wrong. He continued with the vocal as the music swelled.

Lady Queen
You became a friend
You became a friend to me

You tried to make me see all the possibilities
The things that could and should be
Of the journey in front of me
You turned it around you turned it around
Turned it around for me

The final guitar riff soared. Ralt thought it a bit corny, but he knew his father was doing this song as if he had an orchestra behind him, wanting it as majestic as he could make it. Mikal looked up as he did a preliminary mix. The man was wearing a painful grimace.

Ralt saw it, too. "What's his problem?" He looked at his father. He then spotted the queen who wore an impressed smile.

Uasar approached the two. "That was for me?"

"Yes." Mikal replied. "I just thought it would be nice to do something. You did give me a lot to think about."

"If that is my reward for making you think, I shall have to do it more often." Uasar chuckled, gave the father and son an appreciative bow of the head and then left.

The heavyset being waited until the Queen left before speaking. He was not pleased. "I don't see why the queen would be pleased!" He snarled. Even the man who was shaking his head while they were recording was shocked. Apparently, he didn't think it was that bad. The man spoke again. "It was a hideous noise that should have insulted her! The king should beat this nonsense out of you, mix blood!

Mongrel filth like you can do nothing for the king, or Aboria!" He furiously stalked away after spitting on the floor.

The crowd murmured loudly. A few couldn't believe that this man attacked someone who just pleased her majesty.

"You ungrateful bastard!" one woman shouted after him. She turned to Mikal and Ralt. "I don't understand everything you did, but you meant it from your heart, and that is a lot more than he'll ever do!" She looked around and saw that a lot of people were nodding their heads in agreement. "I liked it." There was applause.

Mikal smiled as he looked at his son. He considered his words and then spoke. "Look, I know my father and I didn't start off on the best of terms. I don't love him, but I don't hate him either. I guess you can call it indifference. That's all I can give someone I don't respect." He scanned the faces in the area. "It doesn't matter to me that he is a king. It doesn't matter to me if he has that crown, or the money or the power. Respect should never be beneath him, especially for his children. It's too bad I'll now have to treat him with the same lack of respect he showed me. I do to others what they do to me. That's the law above all law. Treat people with the respect you demand. My father didn't do it, and now it's this big mess." He looked at his son. "A real man will treat his son the way he wants to be treated, like a king."

Mikal went to the machine, pulled the disk out, and put a fresh one in. The crowd murmured again. Something was going to happen. Mikal cued it up and made sure that everything would be in sync. This one was going to rough.

"Son, this is in common time, G major chords and relative chords as well." Mikal said. "Give me deep funk on the base with serious blues throughout. Sound it for me." Ralt did so, knowing his father was pulling the nasty rabbit out of the hat; he reached into his Bootsy Collins bag of tricks with little bit of Larry Graham shot through it all. Mikal's guitar seemed to go completely gut bucket and nasty and for the drums he simply turned on the machine with a simple four-four time. The crowd could hear it, feel it in their bones. They never heard the like before and some of them were bobbing their heads.

"FATHER"

Where were you when I needed you?
Nowhere
Did you really have an interest in the way I grew?
No way
Nowhere, no way, who do you think you're fooling?
Ah—
Well, well, Father
You must be proud of yourself
You must think you're so smart
By leaving others with broken hearts

The first bridge was a screaming, snarling rage of pain

coming through the guitar; the onlookers were shocked to hear his heart come through the instrument and the rhythms were more jagged and broken as Ralt followed his father. They came back to the song.

Why were you such a fool to play this game?
Didn't you have any kind of shame?
Don't you know?
What goes around got to come around
Nowhere, no way, who do you think you're fooling?
Ah—

Well, well, Father
You must be proud of yourself
You must think you're so smart
By leaving others with broken hearts
Ah father

What should be right is wrong
You wrote a song that should not be sung
Done things you should not have done
Taken away what was mine?
Now who do you think you're fooling?
Ah—

Well, well, Father

You must be proud of yourself
You must think you're so smart
By leaving others with broken hearts

The second bridge was a mess of scratching howling chords; he put all the pain he could into them. Ralt simply kept with the drum machine and let his father scream the pain out. The onlookers were shocked to hear how a heart could scream through an instrument. Most had never heard it happen before. The song slipped into minor key and slowed down.

Well father
I must say
I got a life to live
You'd only be in the way
Look me up when you've got something to say

Oh, father
Oh, oh, father
Oh, oh, oh father
Oh, oh, oh, oh, oh, oh father
Maybe, one day I can forgive you
Maybe one day I can't
Give yourself a chance to love yourself
(Spoken) Then maybe you can forgive yourself
Fa . . . . ther
Oh . . . . Father

He repeated the chorus three more times and then faded out.

Unknown to Mikal and Ralt, the queen came back in when a young girl went to get her and tell her what was happening. She rushed back to hear Mikal dedicate the song to the king. She listened with the rest.

Mikal and Ralt wiped the sweat off their faces. They knew they would not play aboard the ship again and they relished the experience. The queen motioned them to stand up. The audience broke into loud sustained applause.

They had connected.

CHAPTER TEN

NEW SONG PLAYING

"Ralt, have you been playing my Stratocaster?" Mikal asked, searching the room.

Ralt stuck his head in the door. "No, fa, I've been playing my acoustic." He stuck his head into the room where his father stood puzzled. "Is it missing?"

"Yeah, it's a couple of days before we reach Aboria and I wanted to make sure it's in its case before we land."

"I'm sure some body would make sure it was." Ralt said as he surveyed the now turned upside down room.

Mikal stood arms akimbo. "Damn!" he muttered. The cabin bell chimed. "I was practicing on that thing before dinner...Ralt, get that...and I know I put it in the case next to my bed."

Ralt walked from his room and saw his father talking to himself and answered the door. "I don't think who ever took it can hock it in space." He chuckled as he answered the door. The chuckling stopped when the door slid open to reveal a huge, powerfully built hominid standing six foot even, brutally wide with huge hands that looked like they could crush a man's skull without sweating. In his left hand, held with a tight grim grip, was the missing Stratocaster guitar. In his right hand, looking absolutely miserable, was a slightly, if that word could be applied, smaller version of the big man held by the scruff of the neck. Both were pale blue skinned with long copper colored hair tied in elaborate braids down their backs. They both had broad features. The elder wore a look of deep frustration and anger and he kept throwing rueful glances at the younger.

Ralt could see the younger was in deep trouble.

"Forgive me young lord, for needlessly bothering you and wasting your good time. I must speak with you on an insignificant problem my idiot son has caused." Man and boy dropped to their knees. "We humbly beg entrance." They kept kneeling until Ralt regained his composure and bade them to come inside.

"Stay right here, please." Ralt said. He turned and kept his sigh quiet. He went into the other room. "Fa, I think the Strat's found its way home." he said as he went into his father's room. Surprised, Mikal went to the front room. The moment the alien (not really, Mikal thought, he and Ralt were the aliens) pair spotted him they dropped to their knees.

"May I ask who you are and why you are on my rug?" asked Mikal who looked over at Ralt as his son shrugged.

"I just open de door mon." Ralt said in his best fake Jamaican voice.

Mikal shook his head and said under his breath "I ought to pop you upside one." He turned to the kneeling pair and asked them to stand up.

The two rose. "Forgive milord for disturbing you. I am Boras Cajon and this idiot," he boxed the youngster's ears, "is my son, Coran." He held out the guitar. He heard you play in the grotto on "B" deck and says he had to try to play your, your."

"Guitar...." Coran finished. That got his ears boxed again.

"Your guitar and decided he couldn't live without. So the young fool found out he was to clean out your rooms. When he saw the instrument in its case, he took it!"

Mikal took the guitar and examined it.

"It is as he took it, milord." Boras said in a nervous quaver in his gruff voice. "I have beaten him once. I could do it again if it would please you."

"No!" Mikal shouted, and then he held his hand up when he realized he just shouted. "That won't be necessary." He turned to Coran. "Why did you take it?"

Coran looked as if he could die. He looked away from Mikal and tried to not look at his furious father as he shifted his feet. "When I heard you play, I'd never heard the like. It excited me!" He raised his hands as if he was holding the guitar and playing it. "Power, melody, and the way you played!" Mikal, Ralt and Boras stared at the boy as visible ecstasy played on his face. "You made the wind howl and the thunder crack and the sound of the water in the storm." His lower lip trembled and his head dropped. "I am sorry and I beg your forgiveness. I meant no harm." His voice drifted off he finished. There was a long silence.

Boras finally said, "Does that make sense to you?"

Mikal looked over at Ralt. "Actually, it does." He said that carefully since he didn't want the other man to think he approved of what the boy did. "Weren't you ever hit so hard by something that you had to try it?"

"But not enough to steal!" Boras roared.

Mikal gave him a dirty "you have got to be kidding me" look.

Boras backed down a little. "Well."

Mikal shook his head. He looked at Coran. "You should have asked in any case. I'm flattered." He went into the other room and put the instrument in its case. He went back into the other room and asked Coran, "Can you read music?"

Coran shook his head no.

Mikal looked at Boras. "You know, I think the worst thing I could do is make him learn music along with everything else he has to do. I take it he has to work with you?"

Boras looked at Mikal then at his son. Suddenly, he knew what Mikal meant. Coran would have to learn as well as do his duties. They both knew the boy would have to fit his practice in with everything he had to do.

Mikal smiled at the new light in Boras' eyes. Sometimes

the worst thing you could get was what you wanted. "I understand, milord." Boras said. "The boy does work with me. He has many duties in addition to his schoolwork. He will have to fit it in."

Ralt shook his head knowing just what his father had planned. Coran was about to get what he wanted, and deal with the consequences, and how he might succeed. Ralt knew his father believed that anyone could rise to the expectations, never shying away from teaching his son how to face any challenge. Ralt watched his father do things with nothing for so long that it was second nature. What Mikal was about to give Coran might just show him what he was capable of. It wasn't just music, it was life.

Mikal went to the computer and punched into the database of the things he brought with him and found the guitar list. He looked over to Coran and noted his skin. "H'm, pale blue...." he turned back to the screen, "so we need an orange guitar, method books, and assorted bits and pieces and we have a lifetime of trying to master the instrument." He stood from the desk. "The things I ordered for you should be up in a few minutes. You know, my first guitar was a very cheap acoustic I paid the equivalent of twenty-nine credits. My next one was an electric one. By the way, you're getting an electric solid body version. Anyway, my next one was electric and then I got a four string bass." He looked over at Ralt who was smiling at him. "We also had a small electric piano. When he was four years old, Ralt liked to climb into my lap and help Father play." Ralt rolled his eyes with an exasperated smile. The door chimed and Mikal let in the servant with the guitar. He handed the guitar to Coran and said, "I want to see if you're sincere." There was also an amplifier, headphones, method books and songbooks. "It's an hour a day, without interfering with your schooling or job, understand?"

"I am unworthy, milord." Coran said.

"That's not what I asked you." Mikal said.

"I understand, milord." Coran said with audible relief.

Boras was the one who was truly grateful. He thought that Mikal would be harder on both of them. It was what he knew from all the other high lords. "Thank you milord."

"Come on Coran, I'll show you a couple of easy chords." Ralt took Coran into his room along with the new Stratocaster.

Between the two fathers there was an awkward silence.

Boras sat down and put his head in his hands; it was all too much sometimes. "Ever since my mate died, I have to take Coran on my job trips. This is no life for the boy. He doesn't have the chance to make friends."

"I've been there," Mikal was sympathetic, "It never gets easier, either."

Boras looked at Mikal. "You are not like the other lords."

Mikal caught what he meant. "I wasn't raised to be royalty. I'm just an ordinary working class guy who turned out to have a king for a father. I suppose I lucked out. I hope I never become royalty."

"You are a generous being." Boras said.

"I can only play one guitar at a time. He might as well have one for himself." Mikal said. He put his new personal seal, two rings representing the two worlds he claimed, with wax on the sheet of paper that gave ownership of the guitar to Coran.

"I was a father at eight and ten." Boras told him. "We were mated a year before that. Shortly after my son was born, his mother, Taranu, died from a plague that swept our world." Mikal could hear the pain in his voice. Boras should have gotten over this by now. Mikal could tell Boras never truly dealt with the loss of his wife. "There are times all I can do is think of her. Gods, I wish the mating wasn't so deep."

"Are you a soul mage?" asked Mikal.

Boras looked up at Mikal. "I am half blood with Aborian. My people have mated with the Aborians for a long time. I found I was a soul mage a long time ago. I also found that when I mated, I went so deep I could never separate fully from her." He looked at Mikal. "She too was a soulmage. When two mages mate, their bond can be so deep it is unbreakable." He swallowed. "She is still in my soul."

"I was a father at six and ten. The girl who was Ralton's mother and I were ships passing in the night. We didn't love each other and I had to pay her with my college fund to get Ralt to birth." Mikal smiled. "He's been worth it though."

"Aye, they are, aren't they?" Boras said. Both men could hear the tentative picking of chords come from the other room. He smiled. "The boys are making friends aren't they?"

"Kids can do that." Mikal said. "They are capable of doing something we have so much trouble trying to do." Mikal stared at the floor and then looked at Coran. "Look, in the future, please try not to hit him so much. I mean, we're not perfect and neither are they. I know it's none of my business."

"I hoped if I punished him enough, you would go easy on him." Boras said.

"I'm just glad you came to me first though. It made it easier on everybody." Mikal said.

"Aye," Boras said. Their sons came into the room. Boras looked at his son. "We should go now." He joined his son as the boy put the guitar in its case and zipped it closed. He hefted the bag with the books and things and shouldered them. Father and son bowed in unison. "Thank you."

Mikal bowed in response. Boras and Coran left.

"I hope you know I'm proud of you." Ralt said.

"I'm proud of me too." Mikal said.

"Don't get too proud, though. We still have to get you and your ego off the ship."

Mikal's eyes went slowly to his son. "You want to die, don't you?"

Ralt took off with his father in hot pursuit.

CHAPTER ELEVEN

ARRIVALS AND SEPARATIONS

Mikal, Queen Uasar, Gherrict and Ralton were on the observation deck as the ship pulled into a parking orbit above the planet Aboria.

"Well, there is your new home." Uasar said.

"What do you think?" Gherrict asked.

"I don't know yet." Mikal said.

"True." Uasar said. "Try not to judge us too harshly, Jon, you just got here."

"Considering all the dinner table politics I've seen so far, I can't screw you any more than you already have done to your selves."

Uasar looked out the windows. "I understand you want to drive yourself to the palace. Why?"

"I just want to see as much of the planet as I can before I get into whatever the king has in store for me." Mikal said. "Besides, it's good to get an idea of where you're going to live. What's wrong with that?"

Uasar frowned. "If you're not careful, you could run

afoul of any law enforcement. You are not known here. Even if you were known, you would have a harder time of it. I don't know how we will deal with it. People have been disappointed with the previous failed attempts." She looked at him. "I don't want you in any trouble, yet."

"Heard and will be obeyed, Majesty. I don't like the idea of running afoul of the law, either. I will be careful." Mikal said.

Uasar was clearly unhappy about this. "I suppose that will have to do."

Gherrict smiled, assuring. "I will be going with him, sister. If he obeys the speed limit, watches himself, he should get to the castle in good time."

Uasar sighed. "I still wish you would speak to the media, it would give people an idea of who you are."

"Which is why the last two guys got screwed. They couldn't handle the pressure and the expectations, and people got tired of photo ops." Mikal was firm. "This whole thing is like a poker game. You don't call the hand before you start playing. I don't have any cards yet, I need to get to my position first, and I need to know the lay of the land." He looked at his stepmother. "Jatis and Brok were blindsided because people knew too much about them." He looked out the window as the ship took its orbit position. "I want nothing out there before I'm ready to give it."

"Be careful, Jon, that could leave you vulnerable." Gherrict said. "You could leave your flank unprotected."

"Yeah, that is a possibility." Mikal mused. "But what we need right now is no undue anticipation of me. We need to have the space for me to operate."

"What if the opposition has a superior hand?" asked Uasar.

"They won't if you haven't told them." Mikal said. "Besides, I want to start small. You've got to remember, I've got to build up a following. I am not going to start at the top where I can be knocked down because I've got no support. I need a cushion for the fall."

Uasar and Gherrict smiled at each other knowing Mikal was hooked.

"You changed your mind about staying, then?" asked Uasar.

Mikal looked at her with a smirk. "Like you didn't know I'd be staying."

Gherrict patted him on the shoulder. "It will be interesting to have you here nephew."

"Oh, yeah, right." Mikal said sarcastically.

"Uncle Gherrict, what were you and dad talking about the other night?" asked Ralt.

Mikal sucked in a breath, and Gherrict set his jaw to keep it from dropping. Ralt raised an eyebrow. "Is this something I shouldn't know about?"

"Yes." Mikal's voice was flat.

Ralt took the hint. "I guess I'll never know." He muttered to himself.

Mikal leaned over and whispered, "let's keep it that way, shall we?"

"Right," The boy replied.

"Mikal," the queen interjected, "it's all over ship that you gave that boy, Coran, a guitar of his own to learn to play."

"Yeah, I did. Then I put mine back in with the rest of the stuff we brought from home to keep it from happening again." Mikal said.

"Well, I must say it's given you a jump on a good reputation." Uasar said.

"That and bus fair gets you a ride," said Mikal as he shrugged. "Besides, if he actually learns to play it I will be surprised."

"What do you mean?" asked Uasar.

"So far, from what I've seen most of the half-breed kids around here aren't encouraged to do much. I hope his father encourages him to try and gives him the space to practice. I hope the kid has the courage to try."

"You believe he can then Mikal?" Gherrict asked.

"If I didn't, I wasted a perfectly good guitar." Mikal replied. "I think he should have the right to fail at least." He looked at his relatives. "Don't you think he should have the right to fail?"

"It's not that, Jon." Uasar said. "It's just that why would you want a child to fail? Why should they go through that pain?"

"That's part of growing up, my Queen. A child should

never grow up thinking that every little thing they will do will be a great success. Failure teaches more than success at the beginning." Mikal said. "How else do they learn?"

"You mean you would have your son be a failure all his life?" Uasar demanded. "I can't see how could say you are a loving father if you would want that!"

Mikal smiled as he shook his head. "I would be less than a loving father if I didn't let him see that you don't win every game and you don't get it right every time. I call it honesty."

"I call it cruelty. No child should be subjected to that." Uasar said.

Mikal shook his head sadly. "One of us is wrong and I don't think it is me. Let's agree to disagree." He turned to Ralt. "Son, you have learned an important lesson."

"Never argue with a Queen when she's got her dander up?" finished Ralt.

"You simply won't admit that you are wrong, just like your father." Uasar said firmly.

"Ouch!" Mikal gasped grabbing at his heart, coughing facetiously. "Partners, she got me." He fell face down on the floor.

Ralt shook his head sadly and took off an imaginary hat. He looked up at Gherrict and spoke with a Western accent (no mean feat in Aborian) and said, "Whal, I guess Space-going Lil got in him in the weakest part of his body, his haid."

Mikal broke up in spasms of laughter, Gherrict did the same as he roared with glee and Uasar covered her mouth in order not to show her teeth. Mikal sat up still laughing until a lieutenant came up to them, saluted and said, "Majesty, Milords, the captain sends his compliments and bids you to be ready to shuttle to the planet."

"Please tell the captain we thank him and we will be ready." Uasar told him.

The lieutenant bowed and turned smartly on his heel and left.

"Well," Mikal spoke getting up off the floor, "it's time son. Let's go see this new world looks like."

"Right. But you know something Fa?" asked Ralt.

"What?" asked his father.

"I really wish the king was here with us."

The three adults grew quiet. "I'm sure he's with us in spirit Ralton." Uasar said quietly.

"He's gotta do better than that." Ralt said as they headed for the shuttles. "A lot better than that."

The Taurus had been retrofitted beautifully. Its flanks were smooth with small stabilizer wings on the sides and bottom, marking it as a flying car. It had clear, laminated glass steel, laser and projectile proof body panels. It had a more comfortable interior, with the instrument panel modified to monitor the new systems. During their trip, Mikal was trained to pilot the car through an advanced virtual reality training sleep teaching. Ralt got the training too although he was too young for his autopilot's license. Ralt gave a huge "Wow."

"You know what else it has son? A massive crystal optical drive that has my entire record collection on it." Mikal said.

"You're kidding, right?" asked Ralt.

"Nope. They showed me everything they put on this car. 'Q' would have a wet dream to examine this car." Mikal said. "It's a lot more plush than your usual limousine."

"Maybe you could show me what they put into it on the way to the palace." Ralt said.

"Oh yeah. We're going to have a good ride," Mikal said as he rubbed his hands together. Father and son, after clearing customs, made their way to the new car. Gherrict joined them in the car. Mikal looked over and saw the royal limousine and the king standing next to it before he got in. Thail Petron waited for his Queen, got in after she did and drove off.

Gherrict saw the look that Thail gave Mikal. All the resentment was still there despite what was said at the welcoming banquet. Ralt drew in a breath of air. He knew there was still a long way to go between those two. He also thought his grandfather should get over it.

"Welcome to Aboria, Jon." Gherrict said. As they drove off, he said, "let's go, shall we?"

Mikal came back to himself. "Is everyone fastened in?"

Gherrict and Ralton replied affirmatively.

Mikal nodded his approval. "Beatles, Magical Mystery Tour, play."

As the music started, Gherrict smiled. "An appropriate choice, nephew."

"I like it," Mikal replied as he drove off. The Taurus sped off from the city-sized star port to their new home. On the way, Gherrict began to point out sights to his nephews. The road had ground vehicles and Mikal shouldn't have been surprised. You only improved old technology dramatically, you didn't abandon it. There were heavy haulers and personal cars along with those that could fly. The addition of painted signs on the highway for those who flew their cars helped guide them. It was comforting to know there were some things similar to what Mikal and Ralton knew. The sky was an incredible shade of blue; beautiful plumed birds flew in formation overhead heading south.

"It's close to winter," Gherrict said. "We got you here just in time. The winter storms can be difficult to fly through, they are nothing you want to trust your luck to."

"What were those birds we just saw?" asked Ralt as he watched them grow smaller in the distance.

"They are called ha'jara. We consider them good luck. Perhaps your new life won't be so bad after all." Despite the fact that Gherrict could be one of the, and there was no other way to say it, spookiest men they knew, he was doing his best to keep them comfortable with the idea this was their new home. He considered it one of his duties Mikal thought. "There is a lot of good here, Mikal, try and find it."

"I always hope for the best and expect the worst." Mikal replied. "Only way to do it."

"I thought that's what you did normally." Ralt said.

Mikal looked in his rear view mirror. "I thought you did too."

"I guess I wish the king had done it differently, you know?" Ralt said. "You and he are a lot alike, Fa."

Mikal looked in the mirror again. "I don't see it."

Gherrict looked at Ralton. He knew the boy wanted to say something, but was holding back. "You should say it, Ralton."

Ralt looked over at his uncle and had a feeling that he would back him up. Ralt also knew his father would at least hear him out. Everything that Gherrict taught them brought his mental game up, he wasn't as young as he was when this all began. Mikal seemed to sense it as well.

"Go ahead and say it." Mikal prompted.

Ralt cleared his throat. "Well, both of you are stubborn, you both know what you want out of life. You don't like having your plans disrupted by any one, but once you see where it's heading, you know you have to ride it out. You're both pretty good at figuring people out, and you never let others know what you're thinking completely. I think you've gotten over what Aunt Bertha did to you, and you worked hard just so you can show everyone else that you weren't going to allow anyone holding you back."

Ralt looked at his uncle, then back to his father. "I think even taking care of me was an act of defiance since it meant that you would do everything you could to prove her wrong about you."

"That's pretty deep, son." Mikal said. "You've been thinking about that?"

"Yeah." Ralt replied. "I mean, you've made our life so far pretty good. I can't think of a thing I've wanted. I remember when you made that bike for me at Christmas from the parts you found on the street. You worked on that thing for weeks so it would be ready on time at Uncle Donald's house."

"How did you know it was over at Donald's?" asked Mikal.

Ralt wore a sheepish grin. "I followed you." Gherrict roared with laughter.

"Boy!" Mikal exclaimed. "You're a better actor than I think!"

"No, I was glad to get the bike!" Ralt smiled. "He even made a chain and got a padlock so I could lock it up when I went anywhere."

Gherrict went thoughtful. "I do believe it's with the things we brought from Earth." He looked over at Mikal. "I know when we first touched minds there was I reason I liked you, Jon."

"Heh." Mikal snorted. "The fact is, once I got inside yours, I found I didn't have to be scared of you, just get through the training intact. I still can't believe the things I'm potentially capable of."

"A soul mage can be powerful, Jon, immensely powerful." Gherrict said. "The depth of soul knowledge you and Ralt already have is astounding. Your effort to build the bicycle is evidence of the deep love you have for your son and the joy you have in seeing him happy. If we can get you to expand that to others, you will be great and strong."

"Even me?" Ralt asked.

"Even you, and I have seen how great your potential is, Ralton." Gherrict said.

"Hey Fa, do you think we'll end up being as great as Gherrict thinks?" asked Ralt.

"Yeah, I do since everything is possible." Mikal said. "I been meaning to ask you, where did you get that 'Fa' stuff from?"

Ralt looked over at Gherrict and shrugged. "Well, the Queen taught me. It turns out that 'dad' and 'daddy' is real close to the slang words for certain female body parts in Aborian. Just a little dirty."

Mikal stole a glance at Gherrict. "You're kidding, right?"

"As Dorothy would say, you're not in Kansas anymore, Toto." Gherrict said.

"That's just sad." Mikal said.

"When in Rome, Mikal." Gherrict told him. "Besides, it doesn't sound too bad, does it? I'm sure you've been called worse."

"And he has!" exclaimed Ralt.

Mikal looked over at Gherrict. "You want to buy a used kid?"

"No, he hasn't finished with you, yet," replied Gherrict.

"I'm catching it from all sides today!" Mikal exclaimed.

"It's only because we love you, Fa," Ralt said as a range of mountains came into view. "What are those mountains called, Uncle Gherrict?"

"A long time ago, they were called the World's Spine. For some they looked like the world was just waking up destroying everything when it stood." Gherrict said. "They are part of the range called the Cyrats. They extend up to the Northern Frost region, about two thousand of your miles."

Mikal whistled. "They are beautiful."

"Yeah." Ralt said.

"When you're settled in, we'll take a flight over them. The northernmost mountains are volcanic though I doubt we'll see any volcanic eruptions." Gherrict said.

The car entered the foothills. None of them noticed the white sedan that followed them discreetly for the last twenty miles nor heard the driver and passenger have a mostly one-sided conversation.

"Our people are in place, milord," The driver said.

"Good," came the reply, "since he didn't want to participate in the media conference, he's made it easier to see to it he disappears. Are our lawmen ready?"

"Yes, milord."

"Try not to kill the mystic, we don't want him dead and it's not worth the trouble. Just make sure he can't identify you," came the order.

"Yes, milord."

"Begin, out."

The white sedan pressed a signal button alerting the trailing patrol cars to begin. Roughly a mile behind, they accelerated and flashed their lights, catching up with the Taurus.

"Uh oh," Mikal groaned.

"What's wrong?" Gherrict wondered.

"You weren't going that fast." Ralt said. He watched as the driver of the patrol unit got out and came to Mikal's window.

"Well, we got the attention of the local chips." Mikal said. "I'm beginning to think this wasn't a good idea."

"You feel it too." Gherrict said.

"Ralt, say nothing in English." His father told him.

"Yes sir." Ralt forced himself calm.

Mikal lowered the window.

"May I see your papers, please, license and registration?" the officer said.

Mikal produced them as Gherrict watched, wanting to make sure that his nephew did everything right.

Gherrict said, "Something's wrong." The officer went back to his patrol car and checked the papers. The officer scanned the bar code in and waited for a moment. The computer beeped.

"It's them. Take them, now."

"Your will be done, milord." The officer gave a small

nod to his parent and the two men got out palming small aerosol tubes in their hands. Once at the car, the first officer ordered Mikal out of the car. Mikal looked over at Gherrict who nodded slightly knowing they were in trouble. None of this felt right.

Mikal got out the car slowly and asked, "Is there anything wrong officer?"

"Yes there is." He sprayed Mikal in the face, and Mikal went down, choking. Gherrict tried to bolt from the car but got a blast from the other officer's spray. Gherrict's abilities fought the effects, but Mikal hadn't advanced that far yet and he lay unconscious on the ground.

Ralt screamed as the elders were attacked. Both officers sprayed the inside of the Taurus and Ralt went down.

"These are supposed to change our world, huh?" The first officer said. "Not after we're done with them."

"A fine lot to be catching, eh Halcon?"

"Yeah, Braal. A pair of poor fish for us but a prize for his lordship." Halcon said. "Let's get them bound and gagged." He looked up. "Here's the hauler." The two tied up Ralt and Mikal as the Taurus was hauled on the carrier. Gherrict, who still lay trying to catch his breath, could hear them and could do nothing.

Halcon looked at the unconscious Ralt. "The boy ought to bring a fair price."

Braal looked over Mikal. "This one doesn't look like much, does he? I saw the video of him striking the king. You would have thought he'd get a lesson right then and there about his place."

"The king is getting soft." Halcon said. "After the first two, you would think he'd learn. Well, now he'll get a proper lesson about how the real Aborians feel about this equality for half-breeds nonsense."

"What about the mystic?" asked Braal.

"Leave him there. He's useless anyway." Halcon said.

"You sure they'll be there with the money?" Braal asked.

Halcon smiled. "Have faith. For what we're getting for this we could retire."

The two got in their patrol car and drove off with the hauler.

Gherrict's head cleared after a few minutes. Gasping for breath he pushed himself on his feet. He looked in the distance where the vehicles disappeared. He began to walk. "Halcon, Braal, you bastards are mine. No one calls me useless."

CHAPTER TWELVE

STEEL BARS

The patrol car approached the huge gray structure that was King Trakisar Prison, a depressing, ugly place. Many of the convicts sent here usually died while in there. The car was identified as it drove to the gate and past the next three double electrified gates. The guards on the five story stone towers scanned for any trouble from their vantage points. The retractable bridge from the mainland pulled in and the gate was shut. The place was dead, a pentagon of silence only broken by the brief speculation on who was coming in.

"Lovely coffin for him, don't you think?" Braal asked. "How deep do you think they'll bury him?"

"How deep is hell?" asked Halcon. "You take in our prisoner, I'll go drop off the boy and be back for you in four hours."

"Why me? I hate this place. It makes me feel like I've died. Can't you come back any sooner?"

"You complain like my mother." Halcon said he watched Braal drag Mikal out and take him in the prison in a fireman's carry. He drove off leaving a disgruntled Braal.

Mikal was unceremoniously thrown into a chair in front of Warden Salvos Wipper. "So this is our new princeling is it? I suppose we're keeping him on ice?"

"Of course, alive, he's leverage, dead he's a corpse." Braal said. "Just see to it he stays out of trouble. You might want to keep him from the rest of the prison population. Beyond that, have fun."

"You're sicker than I am." Wipper smiled. He ran his hand along Mikal's face. "Bruised but tasty."

"Halcon's not going to return for me for four hours. Is there any place in here that isn't depressing where I can wait?" Braal said.

"There's the video room, the library and my bedroom." Wipper told him.

Braal sneered. "I don't do toxic waste dumps."

Wipper laughed. "It's so sad you won't vary your diet Braal." He ran a hand along Mikal's face again. "I guess I'll just have to settle for this." After pressing a button, two guards came in. "Take him to one of our finest suites in the basement, deepest level of course." The two guards picked Mikal up and took him away. Braal left knowing what the warden would do and it disgusted him.

The next morning, Warden Wipper entered Mikal's cell with four armed guards. The cell was dark and dank; the room hadn't seen sunlight since it was built. It stank of rust, mold and filth and what facilities there were hadn't been cleaned in ages. Mikal was glad he'd thrown up last night but wished he could have saved it for Wipper.

Wipper was a medium built, pale skinned man with thinning gray hair, watery brown eyes and thin lips. "We must teach you your place." He was handed a whip. He unwound it, cracked it twice and raised it high above his head. He brought it down and it bit into Mikal's back. Ten, then twenty times it bit into Mikal's back. He stopped as Mikal forced his face into his thin pillow. Wipper stripped, showing how aroused he was. Mounting the bloody back, he took his pleasure and got his release. The four guards did the same. One of the guards quickly dressed and brought in a tray of food.

"Eat it, gain your strength back. You'll get nothing more until you do." Wipper dressed, smiling as he did so. "Thank you for the morning's pleasure." He got to the door and Wipper stopped. "Don't take this personally, I hate all half-breeds equally. You have until my next visit. Try to heal some, won't you?" They all left and the door shut with a clang. It was probably the only solid thing in the cell.

Mikal wiped the tears from his eyes. He knew that if he didn't eat, the healing trance would be less effective. He managed to pull to the edge of the bed and pick up the bowl. He ate carefully if greedily. The pain rushed through his body as he lowered his arms. Getting his breath back, he picked up the bowl and finished the food. Mikal drank the warm sour ale and then fell on his stomach to sleep.

Halcon drove Ralton to a sector called Bavos-Haimn, into Bache City. They went to a part of town called the Dogs, a miserable place of gangs and crime, so bad the police never went in without armor and high-powered weaponry. Bache was nice otherwise, with beautiful parks and grand architecture in the more secured areas. Even so, Halcon went deeper to a place called the Search. This was a place where houses of ill repute flourished. Someone got the bright idea to make them legal and tax them. This had the effect of making them useless to the criminal element since they didn't want to have to declare themselves. It did help to keep taxes flowing since they were some of the most lucrative businesses in town and they supported other businesses. They kept a low profile since they didn't want anyone royal shutting them down. Of course, it didn't hurt that many men of royal persuasion were regular visitors. They kept their visits quiet since they didn't want anyone to know.

They also didn't want it known they had children by many of these women. Since they didn't want it known, many supported those children. The houses saw to their visitors' safety since all knew the party would be over for them if something should go wrong and one of those visitors were hurt or killed. Everyone kept his or her noses clean.

Halcon drove into a garage of a house and stopped. He pulled Ralt out and half carried, half dragged the boy up a set of stairs of a large white and dark blue brick old house. On the roof were several satellite dishes that tracked the oncoming car, feeding their signals to video monitors in the office. Nothing came in or out of the building without being seen. The two entered a beautiful, comfortable parlor where several boys lounged around in various stages of undress. They looked with some curiosity at the new boy and the crooked cop. There wasn't one of the youths who didn't despise the cop, knowing he was a partner in the house they all worked in.

Halcon took Ralt into the office of one Kratos Schram who sat at his desk in an open robe. The office window looked out on a well-manicured lawn lined with flowering bushes; gatergadines with their spicy scented heart shaped blooms. The office was, located in the front of the building with a columned front porch with bay windows to either side of the front door. Ralt and Halcon didn't see it and right now they didn't care.

"It's our favorite little peace officer, isn't it?" Schram purred as he watched the monitor with Halcon dragging Ralton by his collar. "He's brought us a new toy as well." He tied closed the robe, knowing the man didn't want to see him naked. It was amazing that he was part owner of this house but didn't indulge himself. He hit a button on his desk. "Leonis, if you're not busy, get in here."

Leonis Perige was sixteen. Being raised by Schram meant almost nothing to Leonis. He hated Schram and hated his life in this brothel. Still, Schram knew he could depend on

Leonis for the youth knew how the wind blew despite how he felt.

Leonis was just getting to sleep. "What does that old slitch want now? I'm tired, I'm sore and I need my rest!" He slipped on a robe and slippers and made his way to Schram's office. "What now, oh queen of us all?" he said as he entered.

Schram smiled at the youth's attitude, not caring what Leonis thought or liked. If Schram wanted something done, Leonis did it if only to shut Schram up. "You know the world would look much more cheerful to you if you had a much better outlook on life, Leonis."

"Only once you're dead. What happens now?" Leonis said.

"We get a new toy today." Schram answered. "He's about eleven standard years old. It's so nice to get a new boy or girl. I hope he learns to cooperate quickly. He's very pretty."

Leonis felt his stomach tighten. More and more each day he wanted to run. But Schram loved to remind Leonis he was legally Schram's for three more years at least. Leonis hated the jobs of "indoctrination" Schram had him to do. Leonis tried to be as gentle as possible with the new ones.

Leonis knew that sometimes a boy would be sold for the money he could bring in for a poor family, especially if they verged on the pretty. It was cheaper than caring for them, and they helped support their families. He saw the monitor. The boy on it looked miserable. "Oh gods, the poor bastard's in

Halcon's hands. Poor little shit. So he's the new boy?"

"Yes he is." Schram said. "I want you to initiate him, of course. You have such good rapport with them."

Leonis took a good hard look at the screen. Something hit him in the pit of his stomach and he held back his comments.

Halcon and Ralt were led by one of the older boys to the office.

As they entered Halcon said, "Brought you a present, Schram. He's prime, I can tell you that. About ten to eleven standard, he should bring in plenty."

Schram stood to his full six-two height. He caressed the boy's face with a soft hand and tilted it up to see it better. "He is beautiful. How much do you want?"

Halcon smiled. "Two thousand, plus a percentage of everything he makes. We can dicker."

"We can go to the hells! The two thousand's enough!" Schram snorted.

"That's why I said we'll dicker." Halcon smiled. "You should know Schram that he comes courtesy of our high lord above us."

Schram's eyes went wide. He stared at Ralt and then at Halcon. "This isn't?"

"Fresh royal bastard half-breed," Halcon said. "This time we got to them before any damage could be done. The father's in Trakisar and the boy stays with you. Who knows? He may learn to like his new life."

Schram's face went whiter than normal. Swallowing hard, he shouted as he ran his hands through his close-cropped jet-black hair. "Are you mad? Is he? Do you know what can happen if he's found here? There are worse things than dying you know, and I don't want to find out what they are!"

Halcon calmly grabbed the panicked pimp by the collar of his robe. "Listen you bleeding wound, no one will find out especially if you keep your mouth shut and keep the boy out of the main salon." He smiled broadly at the fear Schram wore, in the tightness of the thin mouth and his dark blue eyes. "Do you really think that his lordship would leave anything to chance? He's got all angles covered, so you can enjoy 'initiating' the boy." He let go of Schram. "Maybe you should do the job yourself. That way if you're caught, you can at least have the 'pleasure' of his 'company'." His laugh was nasty and chilling.

Ralt saw they paid no attention to him. He ran for the door and tried the lock and it wouldn't give. The two men laughed. Ralt didn't want to turn around. Once he did, he saw a smile on the face of the brutal cop and Schram had bemusement on his.

Schram went to his desk and opened a drawer. He pulled out a whip about two feet long. "Leonis let's see our new pet; strip him."

Leonis went to a trembling Ralt. "I don't want to do this, but he'll whip us both if I don't. I'm sorry." He whispered. "You shouldn't be here." He took Ralt's clothes and put them in a bag. Leonis then stepped away from him and fought back his tears. You've screwed up big time, Leonis thought. I hope I'm there when it goes wrong. He turned his face from the intense "inspection" Schram put Ralt through. Halcon simply looked bored having seen it several times before.

Schram caressed Ralt's face. Ralt quickly, firmly sank his teeth into Schram's hand.

Schram jerked his hand away with blood flowing from the bite. He stumbled backward clutching his bleeding hand. "You filthy little bastard! Halcon, tie him down!" Halcon doubled Ralt over and tied him wrist to ankle. Schram raised the whip with his uninjured hand and brought it down saying, "Respect for your betters, which is your key to happiness here! That and obedience!" He brought the whip down again and again leaving red stripes on his body. Leonis turned away unable to watch.

Schram finished and turned to Leonis who wore a severe look of disapproval. "Would you like me to do this to you as well?"

Leonis swallowed hard, he'd enough whippings in his life, especially from Schram. "No."

"Good. Get him cleaned up. In two days, the little bastard owes me." Schram said. Everyone knew what that meant. Schram would take him for the first time. After that, he was fair game for everyone. "Heal him nicely, Leonis. Get him close to perfect as possible. Type him and use the plastiskin."

Leonis nodded, picking up Ralt under his arms and taking him carefully out of the room after Schram buzzed the door.

"I'm going to enjoy breaking that one." Schram snarled. "The price is down to fifteen hundred, and you had better believe we'll dicker the percentage!"

"Too bad he's not a full blood. He'd be worth something then." Halcon said. "Anyway, I have to get back to Trakisar and pick up Braal and then I have to report to his Lordship."

Schram wrapped his bleeding hand up tightly. It was dripping profusely and he needed to get it wrapped properly. "I tell you again this is a mistake, a bad mistake. I get a feeling that we're all going to pay for it too."

Halcon sneered, "You complain like my mother."

"At least I know who my mother is." Schram replied. "Yours could have put her womb to better use."

"Bitch," Halcon said.

Schram laughed as he buzzed Halcon out of the room.

CHAPTER THIRTEEN

SEARCHES

Two months later, in the Aborian month of Adve, King Thail Marius Patron paced in his study surrounded by his advisors. His secretary sat at the small desk, hands over her computer keyboard ready to record anything said in the room. It was anachronistic to be sure, but Thail liked the sight of someone other than the life-bonded group of officials.

"So," Thail was impatient, "you've found the corpse of the car, did you?"

"Yes, Majesty, but it was completely stripped." Broman Hav said. "Even the paint was gone. It is my thought that only someone among us could have set this up so well."

Thail stared at him. "What do you mean, Hav?"

"Only you and I knew the route the boy was to take." Hav said. "I gave you the only other copy besides Mikal of his route."

"Hav are you telling me that someone got those maps before we left?" asked Thail.

"That is the only answer I can think of, My King." Hav

spoke with a great deal of apology in his voice. "There were four ways to the Palace Royal. When I spoke to the prince, he wanted the most scenic way to the palace. He said he wanted to get a feel of the planet; a part of it in any case."

"So he took the old Palace Road." Thail mused. "That fits in with what Gherrict said."

"It's a pity that Prince Gherrict isn't here to aid with our investigation." This came from Azol Ornil.

"I know you don't like my brother or his ways. So I will thank you in advance to keep that to yourself." Thail was irritated. "Were he here, he would have your throat and you know it."

Ornil bowed his head. "I beg your forgiveness My King."

Thail waved it off. "Anything on the two police officers that Gherrict mentioned?"

"Braal and Halcon, Majesty," Ure Sterol answered. "Both veterans with spotless records so far. I have my people on the street looking for anything odd. They seemed a little too clean."

"Explain." Thail said.

"Forgive me, My King. But when something's too clean, you are doing nothing or you've worked very hard to clean something up. According to Prince Gherrict, they mentioned money and something about Young Jon bringing a good price. That tells me several things. One, they may still be alive. Two, if they are still alive, this may be something of a hostage play. Three, whoever has them gets what they want and the two are killed." Sterol told him.

"Gods no," Thail said.

"The fact there has been no demands yet might mean that whoever took them may simply be waiting for the right time to kill them to make a point." Ornil said. "It may be the actions of a group who want him to fail like the other two."

"But to hold them for two months is a little too much. Why hold them that long?" asked Thail. "There should have been demands by now." He began to pace again. His eyes caught the look Ornil gave him, but it passed from his notice quickly.

"There is one other thing. The person or persons must be powerful if they can set this sort of thing up." Sterol said. "They had up to the minute access and information. There can be no doubt someone doesn't want what you have in mind to happen."

Thail stood and paced. "It could be anyone of us, even in this room." His voice was heavy. "I never meant for this to happen to him. Mikal will be found, is this understood?"

"Yes, majesty," the three men chorused.

"You are dismissed." Thail told them as he looked out his office window. The three advisors and the secretary left the office as a guard came in and stood silently to the right of the door. "Stand outside." The guard bowed and left, leaving Thail alone as he felt.

He didn't like it, and he knew he needed to talk to

someone. He needed to talk to his queen.

Thail found Uasar in the south royal garden. She was with a group listening to one of their daughters, Resla perform a poem she wrote. Thail listened to his second child recite. Resla was beautiful like her mother with the same heart shaped face, full lips and bright eyes. She had his white hair though, and made her look older than her years. Resla's voice ebbed and flowed with the emotion of the piece. When she finished, her audience and her father applauded and he kissed her on her cheek, his face glowing with pride. "Well done my daughter, an excellent performance."

"Thank you papa," Resla said as she kissed him on the cheek. "I didn't know you were there."

"I just arrived toward the end of your performance. I'd like to hear it in its entirety." Thail smiled. "However, I must borrow your mother."

"Is there anything wrong?" asked Uasar.

"This should be discussed alone for now. Walk with me my wife." Thail said. He saw the looks on their faces. "Don't looks so grave my dears. It is only for the moment, no one will die, I hope."

"You don't know what you're in for. That poem takes a half hour to perform and has twelve characters." Uasar told him.

Thail looked Resla. "An epic. You should have help."

Resla smiled. "Why do you think the others are here for

papa?" Thail laughed heartily. Resla hugged him saying, "It's good to hear you laugh again, papa."

He kissed her on the forehead and then turned to his wife. "Come with me, my wife."

Uasar took Thail's proffered arm and walked off. Resla looked at the others, wondering what was going on as she began telling them about the upcoming performance.

As they made their way through the garden, Uasar felt the tightness in her husband's hand, not in the grip, but in the muscles. She didn't like it. "What is bothering you Thail?"

He didn't answer. She didn't like that either. Uasar stopped, letting her hand slide away from his.

Thail stopped and turned to face her.

Uasar knew that he couldn't, at least not to her. "I'm not the one you have to talk to. If and when you see Mikal next, I hope you try to be man enough to talk with him. I know I've waited long enough for you to tell me what you feel." She caressed his face. "I do love you though, even when you act a fool." With that, she left to rejoin her daughter.

Thail Marius Petron stood alone in the clearing feeling empty, his pride no longer sustaining him. He found it hard to breathe. His chest grew tight with the realization that he didn't really know his wife or his children in or out of his marriage. The children of his marriage and his bastards knew each other. They held open the lines of communication he never established. He barely knew any of them. Yes, Resla would perform the poem for him. He was her father, but he wondered if she truly felt anything for him.

He barely remembered it was Resla he spoke to. How many sons, how many daughters from Uasar? How many outside of his marriage? He didn't know. It was his wife that searched out the bastards.

No, he was the fool who went through his wife's records when he'd found out she did the work of keeping track of those outside children. His truth was clear, they were just names to him with no faces to go with them.

Thail felt his palms were sweaty and cold at the same time. His body was fevered with chills, all of it catching up with him.

He was chosen to rule, but did he? After all, he didn't know the names of his children, he realized he barely knew his wife.

You're some king, he thought. You can't even rule yourself. Lust and passion holds you in a death grip. Why were you afraid to commit to anything?

He couldn't answer.

He already knew the answer. He didn't want the responsibility and he didn't want to fail. But didn't he fail worse by not trying at all?

Yes, the answer screamed, yes he already failed everyone and everything.

Most of all, he failed himself and lost everything that should have mattered.

Thail was on his knees now and he stared at his hands seeing the faces that had no names and hearing the names that had no faces. He frantically rubbed his hands on the ground trying to get rid of the vision, but they wouldn't leave. The rubbing got more frantic and he started to sob uncontrollably. There was nothing he could do about it except curl up in a fetal ball crying, wailing out his grief at what he'd done to himself and his family.

It took a long time for the sobbing to stop.

"Child."

Thail looked up and saw the glowing figure floating just above him a few feet in the air.

"Child," the figure said again, "do you know me?"

Thail's tears stopped and he rubbed his eyes not wanting to believe what he saw. He stammered, "From lesson tapes, you are Mallot," he choked, " Mallot al-Petron, father of us all."

Mallot nodded his head in approval. "At least you know something. What else do you know?"

Thail hung his head in shame. "I don't know them."

"You don't know who? Speak up."

Thail's voice dripped with shame. "I don't know my children, I don't know my wife and gods help me, I don't know myself. I am empty, I am void and I am scared of that. Help me, please."

Mallot nodded grimly. "Well, it's finally come around and you only had to lose three sons to find out what everyone else knew. You are a joke, Thail Marius. If I'd known the line would come to you, I'd have chosen celibacy. Still we must work with what we have. Get up. You may come out now, Gherrict." Gherrict did so, stopping before the two figures and bowing before Mallot. "From the first, the ruling house has been blessed to hear the voice of the past in the present. The mystics of House Petron have guided all rulers since me."

Thail's eyes went wide.

"The house mystics have never been useless, no matter what you or anyone else has said." Mallot continued. "They have sought only to see to it that only the best was ever done for Aboria."

"Brother, I was brought here to be your mystic. Since you would not listen, I became your Major Domo and gave the kind of advice you would listen to. Otherwise, I kept silent. I did your dirty jobs and protected your back. I never left you brother, but you left us. To abandon all that you are was your biggest crime." Gherrict looked at Thail and dropped down to his level. "Oh, but you are ready now."

"Thail Marius."

Thail choked, "yes, ancestor."

"Are you ready to receive us?" Mallot asked.

"I can't go on like this. Yes, ancestor," Thail said.

"Six generations of neglect ends here. We will finally have a king worthy of the name for Aboria again." Gherrict said. "We begin now." Gherrict placed both hands to either side of Thail's forehead, who immediately collapsed.

"He will have to have a family reunion after this." Gherrict said.

"The palace is big enough. After this, he should be man enough as well." Mallot smiled.

"I dearly hope so," Gherrict said, "I dearly hope so."

Mikal Jon turned over in his cot trying to sleep. In the months since he'd been Wipper's "guest", he never did manage except for the first night to get any sleep. When he could sleep, he slept better on the floor under the ragged blanket. Today, he gave up the fight with the cot and sat painfully up. The pain was lessening as he found he could self heal. Doing so left him weak, but whole.

Mikal smiled, remembering Wipper's last visit. The fat, sadistic, balding man made no attempt to hide his taste in anything. He could only rape Mikal several times with armed help. It was the only way to do it since he wasn't strong enough to do it on his own. If any convict said anything Wipper didn't like, guards would hold him down while Wipper beat him senseless.

The door opened and in stepped Wipper wanting his way again. By this time, Mikal was willing to risk something he found he could do. He was willing to risk getting killed if he could pull this off, if it meant getting Wipper off his back.

He got the idea as he found his mind leaving during one of Wipper's "visits". Mikal saw glimpses of a childhood not his own. There were battling parents who fought physically and used their son against each other. As the memories came to him, he retained them. Each time Wipper came by, it was a smorgasbord of pain and suffering that Mikal picked the juiciest bits. This time Mikal was ready.

Wipper's guards put Mikal on his stomach and the pathetic man mounted with his usual lack of grace. Mikal quickly let his mind fly from his body and take in the scene. Satisfied Wipper was happily involved with what he was doing, Mikal began.

"Slavos!" the ghostly voice ripped through the foul room.

Wipper looked up and screamed.

"Slavos, what in the gods' names are you doing to that man?! Get off of him boy before you crush him to death!" The apparition of his father screamed as it faded into view.

Wipper's erection deflated like an untied balloon. "You're dead! You're dead damn you!" The terror filled voice was cracking.

The ghostly apparition appeared of his mother and snarled, "you ought to know, you killed us! What are you doing having sex with men any way?" The ghostly woman turned to her equally ghostly husband and screamed, "This is all your fault! If you had been more of a man, he would have turned out better!"

"If I had married better, everything would have turned out better," said the father. "Besides, he was a loser from day one, a useless toilet of a mistake."

"A toilet of a mistake?" screamed the dead woman, "you were no prize yourself! As for performance in bed, I'm glad I stopped at one!"

"So am I," the father returned, "The neighbors would have sued to get us off the street if we'd had one more."

"STOP IT! DAMN YOU STOP IT!" Wipper screamed until he was hoarse. "GO BACK TO THE GRAVE WHERE I PUT YOU! GO BACK!" with that, Wipper collapsed on the floor babbling incoherent nonsense. The guards dressed him and then carried him away.

"Do you mind releasing me?" Mikal asked a departing guard. The guard did so looking at Mikal out of the corner of his eye. When the guard was finished Mikal rubbed his wrists.

"He won't be bothering you no more." The guard said.

"Yeah, it's a bitch when the parents don't love each other." Mikal replied.

Under his mask, the guard's eyes went wide. "You did that to him!"

"Yeah, what are you going to do, throw me in prison?" Mikal replied.

The guard laughed. "Personally, I'd give you a medal."

"I thought you didn't like half-breeds?"

The guard looked at the open door. "True, but I like him even less. It's about time someone fucked him over. You a mystic?"

"Guess the secret's out. What you going to do?" asked Mikal.

"Nothing for now. I have to see what Wipper will do. Just don't do to me what you did to him, agreed?" the guard said.

"Agreed. Besides, I don't want you, I want the asshole who set me up." Mikal said.

"Fine. By the way your food may improve." The guard told him.

"Thanks." Mikal returned. "What are you going to do about the confession we just heard?"

"Might be a good idea if the royal prosecutor hears about it. But I doubt he'll do anything about it since Wipper's well connected." The guard said.

"Right." Mikal said as the guard left, clanging the door shut behind him.

Ralton Jon hated this. Schram had "initiated" him two months ago and as far as the boy was concerned, it had gone from bad to worse.

All of Schram's clients were rich, powerful people, men and women who liked theirs young. Some of them liked them as young as eight years of age. It sickened Ralt to see this really depraved and disgusting side of people.

Ralt tried to run away once. He'd been caught and beaten badly by the enraged pimp. He wasn't killed like some who ran away and the body disposed discreetly. The boy knew it had something to do with his grandfather and whatever Thail had planned. He knew about the two previous attempts,

Jatis and Brok ending bad and Ralt wondered if this he and his father's fate.

For now, something inside told him to stay where he was, and Ralt was learning to trust his instincts more and more.

Ralt was kept separate from the other boys in the stable, and he got Schram's more "interesting" clients. Some were kind, some vicious. Some simply wanted him naked just to look at him, some fondled him. They all paid a premium for the privilege to have a boy his age.

Ralt took up meditation when the house wasn't busy. During those times, his gifts opened to him and he found he liked being able to leave his body for a short time. He could leave the house although he hadn't learned to get far in his spirit wanderings and he would take quick trips to see what he could see. These were the few real moments of pleasure he had in the house.

Ralt kept all of this to himself.

Ralt did form a friendship with Leonis. Both boys found it odd that it happened.

"Then again, it's right we should talk to each other. Why should we fuck each other more than we already are?" Leonis said. He was the only one besides Schram and the clients who saw Ralt in the house. Leonis brought him food and sat and talked with him. The two boys had a major hatred for the pimp and his police officer cohort.

"I hate this place." Ralt said.

"How do you think I feel?" Leonis said. "I was raised here by that scummer. According to him, my mother needed the money she got for me more than she needed me. Most likely, she owed him big time. She was supposedly using drugs when she got pregged with me."

Ralt cocked an eyebrow. "There's an 'and' in there."

"Yeah. He wanted a live, clean birth. He had connections and she'd get all she wanted once I was born. So while she was heavy with me, he kept her clean. She was high an hour after I popped out."

There was a tense silence for a moment. Ralt wiped his mouth. "I'm sorry. It sounds like a bad parody of my life. How can they do this to us?"

"Who's to say 'no' to them?" Leonis asked. "We are talking about judges, rich matrons, merchants, people who can buy their way out of trouble." Leonis stopped for as moment and then said, "Heh."

"What's so funny?" asked Ralt.

"I've more years to get out of here. You may not think it, but I've saved and invested. When I do leave, I can do so cleanly. I've hidden my accounts from Schram, and while it's not a lot, it's enough to buy me an education and let me do what I can to live a great life. I won't be taking it forever, and I don't want to run a house like this."

Ralt looked at him. "You got ambitions!"

"Yeah. But to express those thoughts out loud is dangerous, best kept to myself. Still is a warm thought, though." Leonis said. "But when I leave, I want to burn this place to the ground.

"Do me a favor?" asked Ralt.

"What?"

"Take me with you, or let me hold the match." Ralt said.

They laughed softly since most of the house was asleep.

"You gonna meditate now?" Leonis asked.

"Yeah, it's better than sleep. I want to see how far I can go this time." Ralt told him. "I traveled a hundred klicks in meditation the first time before Schram came to get me for the evening. Now I do it in the morning." Suddenly, it hit Ralt what he was saying. Leonis didn't know he was a soulmage. He looked at the older boy with an unspoken plea in his eyes.

The youth smiled. "Don't you worry, huh? Schram can't use what he don't know about. Happy meditating." Leonis stood, picked up the plates and left. Ralt heard the door lock as he settled into his lotus. As he did so, a thought hit him. Could he find his way to the prison where his father was? He knew where that was and if he could just get there, he could see his father. He sank into his deepest trance yet and left his body behind in the room. The whorehouse was behind him now as he left in spirit, and he searched his mind for the landmarks he remembered from the journey to Bavos-Haimn. It took a while (his sense of time was skewed in his astral form). He found the huge gray walls of Trakisar prison. Silently rejoicing, Ralt sped through the buildings searching for his father.

He found the warden's office and the agitated warden was screaming at his videophone. What was he saying?

"You didn't tell me he was a mystic!" Wipper said. "What he did to me I can't even describe it! He raped me!" It had taken the warden a long time to get in contact with his master, and only now did he get to the chance to vent.

"Then that should be the least of his crimes. I'm sure he found it as unsatisfying as you did." the other was saying.

Ralt moved behind Wipper to see who he was talking to. The face on the screen was thin, with hard cold eyes, razor sharp cheeks and a hard thin line for a mouth, topped with tar black hair.

"Ornil, I can't stand him being in my prison, I want him out!" Wipper screamed.

The cold eyes flared slightly. "What you want simply doesn't matter. You shouldn't have been doing anything to him in the first place and I'm glad he kicked your head in. If he's not alive and in reasonable shape when I need him, I will dissect you alive. Is that understood?"

Wipper pouted. "Yes, damn it! Oh don't worry, he'll be alive."

Azol Ornil nodded. "That's a good boy, Wipper. Ornil out." The view screen faded and Ralt took off to find his father.

Ralt flew through the prison level by level until he got to the deepest part of the prison. There was no natural light and the air was foul. Ralt shuddered. Why was this happening and who wanted to do them so raw? Then Ralt remembered. His father had always said people did things for several reasons, fear, greed and love. The first one made sense. Somebody was scared. That had to be the reason for the trouble they saw.

He found his father in the corner cell on the bottom. There were two guards outside his door. In his room in the brothel, Ralt's body cried at the sight of his father's emaciated body with the scars on the back. His badly healed face was recently battered again.

Ralt hovered over the cot. The figure stirred and then sat up looking around the small room.

"Who's there?" Mikal rasped.

Ralt wanted to scream. His father's voice, a once strong tenor had broken into a raspy husk of itself.

"Who's there? I know you're there, show yourself." Mikal rasped.

Ralt allowed his spirit to be seen. "Hi, dad." He used English to greet his father.

A swollen eye blinked and the battered face tried to smile. "You're good. Hi son."

"You look terrible." Ralt said painfully.

"Yeah, well, once I mind fucked the warden over, he had me beaten since he can't fuck me."

"That's just a different kind of fuck." Ralt said.

"Yeah, I know." Mikal said. a newly broken rib ground

in him, and that brought tears. He looked at Ralt. "Hey don't cry."

"I can't help it!" Ralt shouted. "I hate this place, I hate this world and everything about it."

Just then Mikal slipped out of his body and joined his son in spirit. He embraced the sobbing boy and held him close. "Now that we touched, I know where you are. I know what you've seen and heard. I don't know how, but we're gonna be all right. Somehow, someway we're gonna be all right." He kissed his son's forehead. "Get back to your body, if it's discovered...."

"It's okay, the door to my room is locked." Ralt told him.

"That's all well and good, but the pimp has the keys." Mikal said. "Get back there."

"Yeah, but what do we do now?" asked Ralt.

"You know all the cliché about the shit hitting the fan and all hell breaking loose?"

"Yes."

His father's spirit smiled. "They will be sorry they screwed us over. Now that I know where you are, I can get to you. I got the warden off my back and I can get my strength back."

Ralt smiled.

Mikal rejoined his body and felt all the pain in it anew. He looked up at the boy. "I love you, son. Get back." He fell back on the cot and fell asleep.

"I love you too, dad." Ralt sped back to his body and woke up to see Schram staring at him with delight, along with one of the houseboys, Diwra.

"I told you Schram, something was wrong when he didn't answer my knock." Diwra said. "I was right, wasn't I?"

"Yes you were. Now get out so I can question the bastard." With that, Schram knelt before Ralt and smiled. "So, we are a mystic, aren't we?" He ran a hand along the boy's face. "You shouldn't hide great talents or gifts like that, my dear. Why don't you show us what you can do, hm?"

"Fish up a tree, pimp." Ralt told him. "I ain't jumping through no hoops for you."

Schram slapped Ralt, who only smiled.

Schram and Diwra were taken aback. "You are going to do what I tell you, you little bastard, or I'll…."

Schram stopped short when he saw the look in the boy's eyes. Schram stepped back. "Lock this room from the outside. Tell the others they are to stay away from this room and him, is this understood?" Schram walked out of the room backwards. Ralt watched every step the pimp made. Diwra did the same, closing the door once he made it outside.

Ralt collapsed on the floor laughing long and hard.

CHAPTER FOURTEEN

RESCUES AND REUNIONS

Gherrict was proud today. He and Mallot al-Petron's spirit worked for a month to get to this day. Thail Marius Petron wore his soul rings. He was now worthy of the title "king".

Thail rose from the kneeling position and addressed the smiling pair. "Now we'll see how well I've learned. Gherrict, I want a meeting with my three top advisors."

"That would be Hav, Ornil and Sterol." Gherrict said. "They were the only royal advisors on the ship."

Thail nodded. "Exactly. All of them life bonded to me. All of them with my deepest trust. One of them has betrayed me ever since I decided that we needed to do something about our so called 'breed problem'." Thail put on his shirt and then his coat. His face was grim. "Our people have been divided against themselves for far too long, and I've been afraid to be a king. In order to rule a world, you first must rule yourself. I never did that." Gherrict and Mallot knew he wasn't talking to them. There was anger in his voice they never heard before.

Thail looked at them. "I have betrayed myself and my people. I have betrayed my sons by demanding they take on a task not even theirs and not giving them the tools or the support to do what I asked. I want my sons back. I will begin with Mikal Jon."

Mallot looked at Gherrict, and then said, "Mikal struck you." Mallot said.

The look Thail gave them told them everything changed. "He didn't strike me hard enough." He pulled the coat tighter around him and left.

"He's a king," Gherrict said, astonished.

"Go get his life bonded advisors, child, before he comes looking for you." Mallot told him. "I can feel him tapping into me and the other ancestri."

"I'm glad we didn't give up on him." Gherrict said.

Gherrict found his brother outside the palace chapel.

"I'm going to pray. I haven't done that in a long time. I need to. I'll see my advisors afterward." Thail said.

Gherrict placed an arm around him. "I'll join you. I've waited a long time to hear you say that. The advisors can wait." They entered the chapel together.

Mikal Jon was meditating ever since Ralt's visit. He was visited by many of his ancestri, both Terran and Aborian. He used the meditation to heal. His single greatest moment of healing came when the spirit of his mother, Sandra, visited him. She appeared at his lowest ebb. The glow surrounding her was warm, powerful. She smiled at her son. "Hello, baby."

Mikal turned to the voice and a huge grin spread on his face. "Ma, what are you doing here?" He stopped and then said, "What am I saying? Why shouldn't you be here? You're probably the biggest, deepest part of me."

Sandra's smile grew larger. "Well, that's nice to hear. How are you?"

"I'm better now." Mikal said.

"That's not what I asked." Sandra said.

Mikal looked at the floor. "I'm healing, trying to figure where Thail and I went wrong."

"So you are just about where I think you should be."

"I don't get it?" Mikal said.

"You are just like your daddy. Only now he has gotten what he needs. Just like you." Sandra told him.

Mikal thought about it for several moments. Then his eyes lit up. "You mean he never had the ancestri?"

Sandra nodded.

"So he put three in the line of fire and he didn't give the first two what they needed because he didn't have it. Damn, Sam." Mikal said. Sandra nodded again.

Mikal stood. "So, Jatis and Brok. How do I know their names?" Then it hit him. "In the ancestri, my entire line is connected. That means those closest to the situation are closest to me. Whoa."

Sandra nodded again. "You know all of this because?"

Mikal looked at his mother's spirit. "Because I'm a

soulmage, those that know their blood all the way to the beginning of their line. We are granted abilities from that knowledge and acceptance of that knowledge. Wipper can't truly hurt me because I know him better than he, don't I?"

Sandra nodded again.

Mikal could feel healing flow through him as he came to truly know what it all meant. Gherrict had only two weeks to teach him about the ancestri and most of it was learn as you go. Even some of the most accomplished soulmages never truly learned it all. Mikal sat down again. The potential of great power was there, as was the potential to abuse that great power. Mikal knew there was more to this now. His potential was enormous and that was terrifying. Mikal knew he now had the power to change so much and he had to get out of there. But something told him to wait. There was something that had to be done by his father, a step to his redemption.

Mikal looked at Sandra. "I understand now."

"I know you do, baby."

Sandra smiled. "I've seen Ralton. He's beautiful."

"All grandmothers say that."

"All grandmothers are entitled to. If I can't think my grand babies are beautiful, how can I spoil them?" Sandra replied. "Reach out your hand."

Mikal did so and felt a power flow through him. It was different from the healing that he felt.

"When you need it, think about me."

"I do that anyway. I'll just keep that in reserve."

"Smart ass. I'm going to visit that grandson of mine. Get busy. I want you out of here." Sandra said.

"So do I, ma." Mikal said.

"You got some new gifts, so use them right. Don't ever use them in anger. That will get you started toward evil. I don't ever want you going that way, you understand me?"

"Yes'm," Mikal said, "I'll try to remember that."

Sandra kissed her son and hugged him.

"Ma, I still miss you."

"Well, you've always had me in your heart. You've got me in spirit. Baby, I never left you. As long as you remember, I'll never leave you." She stepped away from him. "Get back in your body." She watched him do so. "I love you, baby."

"I love you too, ma." Mikal said as Sandra faded from view.

Mikal went into the deepest healing trance possible.

Ralton was under a heavy set, sweaty man who was short of breath and any discernible technique, and he was trying to get Ralt to look at him, and the boy fought him. Furious, the man grabbed Ralt's hair and tried to turn the boy's face to him.

He got the shock of his life. Ralt looked like he did as a boy.

The man withdrew quickly, dressed and left, throwing money on the table next to the bed as left.

Ralt burst out laughing as Sandra, also laughing, came

into view.

Ralt had to think about for a moment until he remembered the photos his father had. "Grand mama?"

She held out her arms and he joined her in spirit and threw his arms around her. "Grand mama, grand mama"

Sandra held her grandson and said, "Shh, shh, it's all right baby, it's all right."

"How did you know where I was?" Ralt asked.

"I've just come from seeing your daddy, when I touched him, I found out where you were." Sandra told him. "From the time you were born I always wanted to hold you." She kissed him. "You were a beautiful baby."

"Grand mama, can you tell King Thail,"

"What's with this 'King Thail' business? That man is your grandfather, don't you forget that."

"Yes'm. Dad always said you were strict."

Sandra cocked an eyebrow.

"Can you tell the king where we are?"

Sandra sighed. "I could tell the king, but he has to make it right between your daddy and him, otherwise it doesn't work. He wronged you, too, and he has to make amends. Therefore, he has to find you. It is his act of repentance. We all have to do them."

"Weren't you mad when he left you pregnant with dad?"

"No; I understood when I joined the ancestri. I could forgive a lot of things then, even Bertha," Sandra explained.

"Well, I'm going to have to leave now, and I'll see you as soon as I can. Now get back to your body."

Ralt did so and Sandra faded from view. Ralt felt stronger, less afraid than ever before. Mikal was right, his grand mama was incredible.

Thail had taps placed on the phones in the offices of his three advisors. All calls were recorded for later analysis. After a week, Thail called his advisors in.

"Gentle beings, we have much to discuss." Thail said as the three men came in. He waited for them to sit in the indicated chairs. Thail picked up a small computer control and pointed at the west wall of the office as four guards took their places in each corner of room.

Thail pressed a button and a screen revealed itself in the wall. "Forgive me, but I had to tap your phones to see who you were calling. Only someone in this office could have done any of this. Jatis, Brok and now Mikal, three sons who I had high hopes for in that they could help me reclaim the planet from its own shortsightedness; the sort of shortsightedness that is destroying the planet day by day. Of all the royal advisors, you three are life-bonded with me. Therefore, where I go, you go. Your knowledge of me is intimate." He sighed. "Sometimes I think too intimate."

Hav and Sterol wore puzzled expressions and Ornil wore nothing.

"You know all these things I know. You're privileged to

know them. In the old days I might have been persuaded by clever talk, a sly suggestion. Not anymore." Thail sat down. "Growing up is a bitch, do you know that? When I realized what I had done, I cried like a baby. I hadn't just betrayed myself, I betrayed everyone. That's what our traitor has done. He hasn't just betrayed me; he has betrayed Aboria. When you do that, there is no turning back. Thanks to two investigations, I know what has happened to my son and grandson." He pressed the computer control to turn it on. "I want you to hear the voice of our traitor."

"I don't care if the boy has turned out to be a mystic, Schram. Keep him until I need him. If the father's death doesn't convince the king, the possibility that he might get the boy back alive will."

"If you can't leave him alone in his hole, Wipper, whatever he does to you is justified. He is not for you, period."

Hav and Sterol stood and moved away from Ornil and went to stand to the left and right of their king.

Ornil sat there defiant.

"I want to know why you did this. Two sons you helped destroy and a third you kidnapped to persuade me to give up trying to heal this planet," Thail said as the guards move to either side of Ornil.

Ornil looked at all of them with hatred in his eyes. "Our problems could be solved without these undesirables here. We could be rid of them."

Thail kept his temper in check. "How?"

Ornil sat silently.

"We went through your records. You had plans to offer those half-breeds who would leave free passage to any world they chose," Thail said getting closer to Ornil. "Those who would not leave, you would have new measures designed to increase the pressure on them." Thail put his hands on the armrests of Ornil's chair and got into his face. "You damned fool. During the last five years there have been two-dozen riots for various reasons with the loss of thousands of people in those riots. I am sick of it! The lives mean nothing to you! The destruction of this world means nothing to you! The loss of our colonies means nothing to you! None of it means anything to you!"

Ornil held the King's stare until Thail broke it.

"Do you know where you made your mistake?" Thail asked.

"No, I don't," Ornil sneered.

"You set my sons up for the trouble they face now. I found out I don't like people attacking my family. They are all my family." Thail told him.

"They are hardly your family. You barely know your legitimate family." Ornil spoke defiantly.

"I can correct my mistakes," Thail replied. "You are one I'm correcting now." The four guards now surrounded Ornil. "I am tired of the blood flowing in the streets. Your 'pressure' would sink this world in an ocean of blood and I know you don't give a damn about that, so I will. Take him away as a traitor. Make sure of this; he doesn't have the money to change your minds." Thail and the other advisors watched as Ornil was marched out.

Thail turned to his last two life-bonded advisors. "How did you find the two dirty police?" he asked Sterol.

"We had them trailed. They both made stops at a whorehouse in Bavos-Haimn the first week. We traced them. We then gained access to their banks accounts and tapped their phones. In those accounts were several payments not from their regular pay. One of them, Halcon, brought in several boys. Halcon left, but the boys did not."

"They were added to the stable." Hav said with no small disgust. "I knew we had dirty officers, I just didn't know some of them went for this."

"So this Schram gives this Halcon and possibly Braal a percentage of the boy's earnings." Thail snarled, "And he has been getting a percentage from my grandson's. Let's make it expensive."

Hav began, "Braal is the junior member of this little triad, and he can be taken now. I have the feeling that he and Halcon have known each other for a long time. They may be lovers. Both men have no known relatives or children."

"Take him, and bring him to me. I want Gherrict in on this and I want both of you here when we talk to him." Thail said. "Braal is going to tell us everything."

"Yes majesty." Both men smiled.

The next day, officer Braal found himself in a windowless room in hand and leg cuffs. He'd been taken after a night of drunken partying and his head was a mess. Still he was far more sober now than he'd ever been when he saw the king and his advisors standing in front of him. The king wore grim satisfaction and the advisors were silent. Thail began.

"You are Golnus Braal?"

Braal looked around nervously. "Yes. What is this about?"

"You and your friends have caused me a great deal of pain," Thail said.

"I don't understand, milord. How could I have caused you pain?" Braal asked as panic slowly creeping in his voice.

Gherrict brought a small ring into the lit area Braal sat in. "Do you recognize the coin in this ring?"

"No, milord, I do not." Braal said.

Gherrict looked at it. "It is called a penny, this copper. Lowest denomination of the money in the home nation state of your kidnap victims."

"I didn't know that sir." Braal said.

"It is too bad that it is the smallest value coin. The depiction is of one of their greatest leaders, one Abraham Lincoln, their sixteenth president. Did everything he could to keep that nation together. In the end it cost him his life because someone who disagreed with him shot him in the head while he was at the theater enjoying a play. They have one of the more impressive monuments to him in their nation's capital. I've seen it, it is beautiful." Gherrict walked around Braal, contemplating the ring. "What makes the ring special is that it is of a set of coins from the year of Ralton's birth. Where did you get it?"

Braal knew he was in deep trouble. "I found it" wasn't going to work.

Gherrict could see the dirty cop was thinking and finding no answers out of his situation. "Where is the boy?"

Still no answer and the cop started to struggle in his chair. Gherrict placed a hand on his shoulder and let a shock of energy flow through him. Braal screamed and fell forward.

"It can get worse," Gherrict said. "Especially if the king does it and he is angry. He should never use his powers in anger. Me, I just want to find my nephews."

Thail stepped toward Braal. "Where are my son and grandson?"

Braal sputtered, "You know where they are or you wouldn't have found me!"

Thail got into his face. "Confirm it for me."

Braal shook when he looked into Thail's eyes. If he was a soulmage, he could kill him just by looking at him. "The father's in Trakisar. The boy is in a whorehouse my partner co-owns. They figured the boy ought to earn his keep while we held him." That got him a hard slap from Thail.

"If anyone finds you, it won't happen." Thail stepped back. "Take this trash to our prison colony planet, Avairdus-5. I want him buried." Two guards came in and dragged him away. "He ought to have as much fun as Ornil does now that they'll share the same planet."

Gherrict said. "I'll go get Mikal. We have to keep this quiet. Our people are in place."

"Good. Have we got Ornil's contacts out of the way?" Thail asked as he left the room with the others following.

"Yes, Majesty." Hav said.

"Good. Have the whorehouse watched and get ready to take it. I want you there, Gherrict. No one is to leave it or the prison. Get my sons." Thail said as he went to his office, leaving Hav, Sterol and Gherrict standing in the corridor.

Hav smiled. "He's a king now. I like it."

"So do I." Sterol echoed.

Gherrict merely laughed as they left.

Wipper was gone.

Gherrict stood in the office and reached out for the warden. He found Mikal. The troops surrounding the prison made it clear they would put anyone down attempting to make an escape, and Wipper knew it was over. Wipper fled to Mikal's cell to kill the one he blamed for his downfall.

The prison grapevine was abuzz with the news of the activity in and around the prison. One of the honor inmates saw the rotund Wipper running as best he could to his special elevator and going down in it.

Despite his healing trances, Mikal was still weak and Wipper knew it. He saw to that by keeping him underfed.

Wipper believed it would be easy.

On the fifth level, Wipper went straight for Mikal's cell, carrying a weapon called a needle gun. It fired needles that could shred a man.

Sweating profusely, Wipper steadied his shaking gun hand and checked the cell. Mikal was meditating.

Wanting a clear shot, Wipper opened the door, took aim and pressed the trigger. The shot went wild and Mikal keeled over.

When Hav and Gherrict got to level five, they saw the late Slavos Wipper lying in a pool of his own blood with the back of his head missing. Looking inside, they saw Mikal lying on his side.

"Gods, no!" Gherrict stepped over Wipper's body. Rolling Mikal on his back, he checked for a heartbeat and found it. He sought Mikal's spirit. "Too early to join the ancestri, respond to me."

Mikal coughed and his eyes struggled open. He saw Gherrict. "I . . . am . . . so . . . glad . . . to . . . see . . . you." he rasped. Gherrict lifted his nephew and carried him out of the cell.

"Milord, what do we do with the warden?" Hav asked.

"Flush it." Gherrict said as he carried Mikal to the elevator and out of the prison.

At the same time, Sterol and a group of Royal Guardsmen also surrounded Schram's. Sterol went to the front door and knocked.

A young man, who looked to be twenty, answered it. "May I help you?"

"I'd like to speak with the master of the house." Sterol said.

"He's not in."

"MILORD, SOMEONE TRYING TO LEAVE OUT THE BACK WAY!"

Sterol pushed his way past the youth and into the house. "Where's the office?" He demanded.

A panicked younger boy pointed upstairs.

Sterol told the guard to his right, "See what records you can find. The guard went upstairs and Sterol went to the rear of the house.

"You've ruined everything!" Schram screamed. "Well, I'm not going down by myself, you'll be dead before I am!" He pulled a wicked looking Dagger and raised it above his head and started to bring it down when Ralt heard a thud from behind Schram, whose eyes went wide in surprise. Schram staggered back to see who stabbed him.

Leonis stood there with another knife, hate and contempt burning in his eyes.

Schram stumbled to the outside stairway he was taking Ralt down; he teetered at the top and then fell to the ground in the alley outside.

Sterol arrived to see the two boys staring at the body of the late pimp. "What happened?"

Ralt and Leonis looked at each other. "He made up for a lousy summer."

"….Of course." Leonis finished.

It was a few days later that Gherrict and Leonis parked outside a rundown apartment building.

"This her last address." Leonis said.

"I've checked, it's her only address." Gherrict said as he took his briefcase with him. "Shall we?'

They went to the door and knocked. It opened on an apartment that held a great stench of old cooking and trash that hadn't been moved for quite some time. The woman who answered the door was a mess of badly patched clothing, stringy gray hair and missing teeth. "What do you want?"

"Are you Tera Perige?" asked Gherrict.

"Who wants to know?" Tera said looking at the tall man with the blood red eyes.

Leonis stepped from behind Gherrict. "Answer him."

Tera stared at the both of them. "He's your new pimp, then?"

"No, he's not." Leonis said and he pushed his way inside. He wrinkled his nose. "Don't you ever open a window?"

"What do you care?" Tera said. She looked her only child over. "You got fancy new clothes now. I didn't know the pimp was paying you that much."

"Schram's dead," Leonis said.

Tera grunted a laugh and sat down in a ragged chair. "So who did it?"

"I did," Leonis told her.

Tera smiled a gapped toothed smile. "You know he was your father, don't you?"

"After I found the papers, yeah." Leonis said. "I'm amazed you actually got together."

Tera turned her attention to Gherrict. "Why are you with him?"

Gherrict pulled some paper out of the briefcase he carried. "This entitles you to a stipend of fifteen hundred credits a month; it will not affect your dole."

Tera looked him with suspicion. "Why are you doing this?"

"Leonis is moving in with new guardians. This is to help you so you don't miss what you were getting from the late pimp." Gherrict told her.

Tera looked at them both incredulously. "This is mine? As long as I don't make no noise, right?"

"That would help," Leonis said.

Tera smiled widely and they could see her missing teeth. "I just sign and I get free money for staying out of your life, eh boy?"

"If that's the way you want to put it, yes," Leonis replied.

Tera turned a bloodshot eye to Gherrict. "You got a pen?" she laughed.

Gherrict handed her one and she signed where she was told. She handed the papers back and Gherrict handed her a card with her name on it.

"I suggest you pay your bills first and the rest is play money," Gherrict said.

"Pleasure doing business with you, milord," Tera said with some glee as she examined the card.

"Let's go," Leonis said as he went to the door and opened it and walked out.

"Such a good, good boy!" Tera laughed as Gherrict followed Leonis.

The doctor insisted on a week's rest before Mikal had visitors. Gherrict and Ralton visited him in spirit. Mikal was healing well.

Thail would only visit his son physically while he slept, his thoughts kept to himself.

A week went by, and Mikal finally went outside into the west garden mid-afternoon sun. The sun was warm on Mikal's skin and he reveled in his freedom after months of forced incarceration. He watched as Ralt gave Leonis a guitar lesson on a lower level. He would have done it himself, but he enjoyed taking the doctor's orders seriously to take it easy.

Thail, Gherrict and Uasar sat on the patio having tea. Thail kept looking over to his son. Several members of the family kept looking at Thail looking at his son, grandson and the new royal ward.

Thail stood and went to Mikal; it was time.

"Mikal," Thail said when he approached the lounging Mikal.

"Majesty."

"I'm sorry, Mikal Jon about everything. I should have told you who I was. I should have talked to you before I brought you here," Thail said."I'm afraid that is all I have to say."

A heartbeat.

Mikal stood up. "Father, are you going to run away again?" He held up his hand. "My name is Mikal Jon Ston-Petron," he pointed to Ralt, "That is my son Ralton Jon Ston-Petron."

Thail took the offered hand. "I am Thail Marius Petron and I am pleased to meet you."

Thail stepped forward and embraced Mikal. Something broke through, and a new power began flowing through them both. It was rich and deep as if worlds were finally acknowledging their value to each other. Mikal and Thail could see beautiful colored light patterns of two worlds surrounding them. Ralton and Gherrict and the other soulmages in the family could see it too. Everyone in the garden could fell the power they stood in. The ancestri of two worlds appeared standing around them smiling.

Gherrict and Uasar toasted the father and son as they embraced as the others applauded.

Ralt looked over at Leonis and smiled. "Welcome to the family, man."

THE END

PRELUDE

LEONIS LEAVES FOR A WALKABOUT

Leonis lived in the palace almost a year. He knew it was not his, no matter how much he loved being there. The palace was beautiful of course with many twists and turns and secret places, but it wasn't his.

Leonis took his guitar and sat on the balcony of one of the towers and looked out. Playing softly, he let the breeze be part of that moment, letting all of it go and just feeling it all. His adoption by Mikal and Ralton was smooth because his mother had no interest in interfering with what was going on. Mikal and Gherrict also helped him achieve his soul rings.

Standing and looking over the vast grounds, Leonis smiled. He was still feeling empty and want to try and fill that space. He'd been unwanted at birth by either parent, he'd been a whore and was glad to be out of that.

Now what? That 'what' wasn't going to be filled by sitting here on a balcony looking at what wasn't his. He needed a new purpose.

He looked at his guitar, a gift from Mikal. He'd learned quickly. While he might never be the most important person to play the instrument, he at least could coax music from it and could passably sing. It gave him comfort and he loved that he could write songs just to feel better.

Leonis laughed at himself. The answer for now was simple. He had to leave. Not permanently, just for a little while. Clear his head and fill his soul. Living in the palace wasn't going to do that. Making up his mind, Leonis went inside.

The next morning, Leonis printed out maps for the roads he would take. He would leave Bache City for a while and see something, anything else. It might be foolish, but he needed a change of scenery. He wanted to see the sights advertised, and it seemed now was a good time to fulfill his bucket list.

Leonis was sixteen standard years old when he and Ralton met, now he was approaching his eighteenth standard year birthday. He had his autopilot's license, he had his stash of money, and he could travel. Yeah, he might be thought mad, but at the least Mikal would understand, he hoped.

As he sat at the computer, Gherrict came in the room. Picking up a printout, he saw it was a map. "You plan on leaving us?" asked Gherrict.

Leonis smiled. "No, uncle of my heart. Just a printout so I can plan a trip for a year. I know within the next year, you're going to have the big reunion, right?"

"Right..."

"So, it will not truly involve me. So I decided to take a walkabout to clear my head and to figure me out." Leonis said.

"You do realize of course, that Mikal at the very least, will kill you for such an idea?" Gherrict said.

"True," Leonis said. "But what I'm looking for needs quiet. It needs me to get inside my own head, and I need the space to do that. It's not here in the palace."

"Trust me, I understand," Gherrict said. "But you are included in the reunion."

"Perhaps. The reunion is about His Majesty throwing off the royal and getting down to the man; connecting with his children. By the very nature of the reunion, I will be excluded. Besides, it's your adventure as well."

"I know these nephew and nieces well and they know me. I might not be at the reunion either." Gherrict said.

"Then there will be two gone." Leonis said.

As they were talking, the queen walked into the room. "What are you talking about?" she asked Gherrict.

He held one of the printouts up. "He's pulling together roadmaps for a trip to take a year."

Uasar looked at the map. "To do what?"

"To talk. A walkabout." Gherrict said.

Uasar looked at the newest member of the house. "You can't do it! The reunion is going to happen in the next year!"

Leonis wanted to bang his head against the keyboard. "Majesty, this reunion is not about me, it is about the king, and Mikal as well. The two of them will be dealing with this huge extended family and I don't need to be there. He's the one that needs it. I need to decide what I'm going to do next. Mikal has to make up his mind how he is going to approach the problems of Bavos-Haim. Your plates are full. I don't need to be there." He sighed. "I love you all, truly I do. But that love isn't enough. If I am to be worth anything to you at all, I have to go on walkabout. I need to be sure of who I am."

"We have places you can go…" The Queen said.

"Yeah with doctors and therapists and drugs and guided tours through my mind." Leonis turned to the queen with a warm smile. "You are the mother of my heart. But this time, I need to leave. I will be back in a year if I have figured myself out. Or at least be on the way to figuring me out." He stood and embraced them both. "Please don't deny me the chance to do that?"

Uasar sighed in resignation. She knew Leonis needed this. "Very well then. How are you traveling?"

"Personal vehicle. I just want to see. I want to experience. You do understand that?" Leonis asked.

Uasar sighed. "I understand. I did the same when I was young, except not as long."

Leonis dropped to his knee and kissed her hand. "Thank you."

"You better hope Mikal doesn't kill you." Gherrict said.

"I'll tell him." Leonis said.

"Make the trip no more than a standard year. I don't

care to wait that long. We might have something you'll like when you come back." Uasar said.

"Yes ma'am." Leonis said as the queen turned to leave.

The queen stopped at the door and turned to face Leonis. "You will inform Mikal Jon tonight at dinner you are leaving. I'm sure he'll have something to say about it." The queen left.

"Well, she's pissed." Leonis said. "She might understand, but she's pissed."

"I'm not happy either, but I understand." Gherrict said.

Mikal wanted to tell Leonis not to go, and he knew it was useless. Leonis, while he was welcome in the place, felt no need to stay there. He saw the small van Leonis decided to travel in. He knew it was stocked with all he needed to travel, and he knew Leonis was ready to go. he also knew Leonis had the money for such a trip. Leonis was smart that way.

Mikal wanted to go.

Mikal was up the next morning to see Leonis off. He was also there to ask him one more time to stay, just as the Queen asked him to.

Leonis put a hot breakfast sandwich on the passenger seat before pulling on his safety belt and starting the engine.

Mikal leaned into the open drivers window. "The queen has asked me to ask you not to go one last time."

"I know," Leonis said. "I have to."

"I know that too," Mikal said. "I just wish I could go

with you."

"I'd ask you, but you got a family reunion to go to," Leonis said. "You don't need me there."

"I do love you and I wish you safe and happy travels," Mikal said.

"Thank you for becoming my new father," Leonis told him. He started the vehicle and Mikal stepped away. Mikal watched Leonis drive off. Mikal stood rooted until he sighed and walked back into the palace.

###

Of Reunions